SINNER'S PARADISE

Scott Lettieri

CREATIVE ARTS BOOK COMPANY
Berkeley • California

Sinner's Paradise is published by Donald S. Ellis
and distributed by Creative Arts Book Company

For information contact:
Creative Arts Book Company
833 Bancroft Way
Berkeley, California 94710
1-800-848-7789

Acknowledgments:
My parents, Josephine and Atillio Lettieri.
My sister Katherine, Paul Costanzo, Christopher Suisinski,
John and Katie Tassinari, and most of all,
Robert Nader, whose key unlocked the door of this story.

ISBN 0-88739-421-3
Library of Congress Catalog Number 2002104808
Printed in the United States of America

SINNER'S PARADISE

For Teresa, my patron saint of love

SINNER'S PARADISE

Life is a dream from which death awakes us.
—Old Mexican saying

PROLOGUE

"Doctor, she won't stop coughing and I think she's in pain."

"She is in the final stages of cancer, Martin."

These fucking doctors, he thought. "Yes, I know that. It's three o'clock in the morning, she's been coughing the last two hours. I called to ask for your help. Now what should I do?"

"I'm sorry. It was good that you called. Do you have any morphine left?"

"Yes."

"Good. Give her two cc's, about a teaspoon full. Prop her head up and make sure you get the morphine down."

"I'm sorry for waking you, I know it's late."

"Don't worry about that now. Just do what I say, and keep her head propped up. Understand?"

"Yes."

"If this continues we're going to have to put her back in the hospital."

"She's not going to die in the hospital, Doctor."

"I know how you feel about it, but your mother is a strong woman. She could hang on for a long time. I think it's just too much to ask of you."

"No, it's just a bad night. We'll be fine. Thank you, Doctor Allen."

She'd be dead soon. The cancer had metastasized to her brain and her frail bones. Dr. Allen said it was a matter of days. Martin had spoken with her minister, her therapist, all her doctors. They had all tried to prepare him. Despite the situation he continued feeding her only "healthy" foods. No meat. No soda. No Kentucky Fried Chicken mashed potatoes, which she said she craved. Every day he made her Sunrider herbal shakes to help with her digestion and immune system. He knew it was futile, but he couldn't help thinking that she was overacting.

Laura Castillo-Fante had always exaggerated. She was a dramatic woman. Even a simple sneeze could be a production: quick breaths through her long, sleek nose. As she closed her eyes her breathing would draw to a crescendo before a guttural gulp of air, then the explosion. The process repeating at least three times before any bystander could get in a timid "bless you." It amused Martin to see other women attempt to stifle a sneeze or make it more ladylike by holding back and expelling a high-pitched *choo!*

Still, he knew she was dying, and he started to get things in order.

His mother had closets full of boxes. Among them were plastic dairy crates she had swiped from behind local supermarkets. Some were stacked full of magazines, newspapers, family pictures, schoolwork from both kids. Others were filled with his mother's degrees and college papers, notes from her practice, outdated insurance policies, bank statements, old books, Christmas cards, and piles of old canceled checks. Normally, Martin hated combing through such stuff, but as he examined each document, paper, picture, he felt comforted. Everything seemed to bring a memory or a feeling. He found a seventh grade report card that he had doctored, changing a "D" in Spanish to a "B." The alteration seemed obvious now, but at the time his mother said nothing. It took half the day to go through all the crates and boxes. The process regenerated him, giving added purpose to the task of caring for his mother, who was slipping away on the living room couch where she felt more "alive."

As a middle-aged woman she had remained beautiful. Even in those last days lying on that gray poplin sofa that always reminded Martin of an approaching storm. Despite being bald, emaciated and removed from her senses, her high Indian cheekbones, full lips, and aqueous brown eyes gave her an elegance reserved for, Martin imagined, an Aztec princess or an Apache maiden.

Going through the last crate he came upon an old jewelry box. It was made of poster board and covered in faded blue lace. He unsnapped the top. Inside were a number of small items along with a sealed envelope with his name on it. Inside was a letter in his mother's handwriting.

Spring 1993

Dearest Son,

In this "treasure box" you will find items I saved over the years. An explanation about the box. When we were newlyweds your dad gave it to me filled with panties for every day of the week. I'm not sure why I saved it, but I suspect that it symbolized the love, hopes, and dreams we shared. The love we lost, but we got a treasure, you. The fish pin you brought back to me from New York. You were eight years old. I remember you still, wearing white bellbottoms and sandals. The spoon bracelet you made for me when you were nine. The gold-plated bracelet your dad bought me when you were a baby. There are various stamps that I saved, one in particular, the first man on the moon. I felt bad about throwing away your baseball cards so I've enclosed some recent ones. You were such a loving boy.

There are many memories I have of you as an infant, how elated and scared I was when I learned I was pregnant. God, I was so young and I used to pray that I'd be a good mother. I blew it so many times. It never had anything to do with you. You were just a kid doing what kids do. The bracelet with the stone, you bought for me. You had it on layaway at that store on Van Nuys Blvd. Cost you five dollars.

I love you, sonny.
May you find peace in your life.
Mom

CHAPTER 1

The *Red Room* is different from other lesbian bars in San Francisco. Far from the gay enclaves in the Castro and Noe Valley, it's located in the bowels of the Tenderloin on Eddy just off Leavenworth. To get to its low-key entrance one has to weave through a labyrinth of catatonic and crazed pockmarked junkies, emaciated AIDS victims, and grizzled, stench-ridden drunk men of all ages. But the patrons, who come from all over the city, are much better off. Or so they think. Ambivalence is the bar's main appeal, along with its velvety lounge furniture bathed in red light. As I entered I felt as if I was walking into a giant vagina. Sitting Bull, James Cagney, Clint Eastwood, Lucky Luciano. When I was growing up these men were my heroes, my role models. How would Harry Callahan feel about walking into a giant vagina searching for a woman he was obsessed with?

I quickly scanned the bar. I sat down to have a drink and plan my next move. The lanky bartender with the eyebrow ring and the Sinead O'Connor buzz cut approached me. "What'll be?"

"Stoli on ice, please."

She brought my drink and turned without looking at me. I took my glass to a lounge chair in the back.

No Sarah. The bar was lined with dykes. Dykes that appealed to her in a way I never could. I took out a small book from inside my coat pocket. D. H. Lawrence's, *Love Among the Haystacks*. Sitting in the shadows, I strained my eyes to read a steamy passage about passion in a barn. Why couldn't I feel the way Lawrence wrote? Emotions popping and writhing. You could knead the sex, smell the desire. Words too dreamy, too unattainable. I began thinking thoughts of betrayal with a vague notion that Sarah knew what was in my head.

We had had an icy exchange that morning. She was already up when I got out of bed. As I made my way into the kitchen I noticed her sitting, feet up on a chair, coffee cup in hand, in just a dingy T-shirt and panties. She smelled faintly of bourbon and sweat. I gave her the once over and immediately got the *don't come near me* vibe. Without thinking I retaliated with a verbal salvo. "Are you working tonight?"

"No."

"How many days did you work this week?"

"Don't worry you'll get your money," she said as she took a sip of coffee.

"I'm not worried. I was just wondering—"

"—Uh, huh. Why should I work today? It's Saturday. Most normal people don't work on Saturday. You don't work on Saturday."

"I've got a full-time job. Besides, I thought weekends were best for tips?"

"Maybe. I'm sick of working on Saturdays. It's too hectic, and now with Fleet Week and all those dreary, adolescent sailors. If Anthony wasn't so goddamned cheap he'd hire and extra person or two for the weekends."

She had moved into my apartment after her hours at the cafe were cut back.

The bourbon and cocaine had taken a toll, but her lean shape, square shoulders, perfect breasts, and mournful green eyes gave her a regal quality. She clung to her princess persona with a spirited bravery I found irresistible. "You know, Monday is the first?"

"Man, you just keep riding me, don't you?"

"Sorry. I'm a bit tapped this month."

"I'll have it."

I was skeptical. If she was on time it would be the first in the four months she had lived there. But I let it go, instead saying, "I know you will, baby. What do you say we take a ride on the Honda to Pier 40 for breakfast? My treat?"

"I'm not hungry."

"It's a great day for a motorcycle ride?"

"I'm not in the mood. You go, Martin."

Sitting in that dyke bar I hoped to catch a perverse glimpse of Sarah in action, like somehow it would give me insight into her aloof temperament.

I had never seen as deeply into her as I expected. Sometimes she'd come close to opening up, like when she talked about her dead father. He had survived two years in Dachau. Before the war he'd been an intellectual in Poland, a professor and a mid-level government official. She called him her Siddhartha. Her mother had abandoned them when Sarah was a teenager. He was fifty-five when Sarah was born. A miracle. He never let her forget that. Seeing him die slowly of cancer embittered her. When she spoke of him, perhaps after lovemaking or a few bourbons her voice would lower to a whisper and her eyes would moisten. But she would always catch herself, turn on me as if I had tricked her into talking and ask, "Do you understand?"

As I looked up from my book I saw Sarah enter the bar, followed by Paige. Blue Paige I called her, always so austere and quiet. Her mousy blond hair was hanging in her eyes. They sat down in a booth against the opposite wall. I sank in my chair, hoping they wouldn't turn and see me. Sarah was beautifully haggard as usual. Paige was as jumpy as a crab in an empty swimming pool, biting her nails and pawing at Sarah.

From across the narrow room I could read their expressions. Paige was over-accommodating. Sarah was coy and distant. On display was that lurid, sex kitten indifference she uses as a bittersweet lure, reserved for those she lets near. I understood then that she and Paige were lovers.

It appeared Paige was making an appeal. Sarah turned away as Paige flapped her arms and jerked her head. After minutes of this, Sarah turned her eyes back toward Paige, staring at her with a soft yet predatory look that silenced the girl. Then she leaned over the table and kissed her. That long, probing kiss reached down into that poor girl's soul. I know that kiss well. I could almost taste Sarah's delicate, firm tobacco tongue. Sarah then gazed off, took a victory drag on her cigarette, and blew long tendrils of smoke toward the ceiling.

I felt nothing. Like when I rewrite wire copy about mass grave sites in Bosnia, parents killing their children, then themselves, or suicide bombings in the Middle East.

Moments later Sarah left the booth and headed toward the bathroom. I left the bar before she returned.

Back in my apartment I felt safe. I poured what was left of the vodka over some vermouth I had picked up cheap at Molinari's. I peed.

Looking in the bathroom mirror I studied the thin scar that runs halfway over my left eyelid and across my temple. The scar is compliments of Henry Guzman's hockey stick. I had blocked the follow-through of his slapshot with my head. The young doctor in the emergency room told the nurse that I was going to lose my eye. I didn't, but the muscle that contracts the pupil was permanently damaged, turning my left eye a darker brown than my right and giving me headaches when exposed to too much light. I remembered the pain of that injury: how I initially pretended it was nothing. But later in the hospital I collapsed, then vomited.

I took a drink and decided to shave. Using just the regular hot water and blue razor, I wondered how many people had killed themselves while shaving, getting drunk and slicing their throat with a straight blade. I scraped hard then washed the stubble down the drain. More of me in the sewer.

The front door opened as I drifted out of a restless sleep. I smelled a stale smoke as Sarah walked in. She staggered to the bathroom, brushed her teeth, then came to bed. Lying on my stomach with my head and arms curled around a pillow, I pretended I was asleep. She climbed in bed naked, smelling of bourbon and toothpaste. Crawling up next to me, she asked, "Are you awake, baby?"

"No."

"Is the big fella awake?"

I couldn't help but laugh. She reached down between my legs then climbed on top of me. While her hands pushed down on my chest and her head tilted up toward the ceiling, I looked up and saw the reflected light of a car from the street below bounce through my window onto the wall.

Chapter 2

And then there was work.

United News Service
San Francisco, California

JOB DESCRIPTION: News anchor/reporter
PAY: Negotiable, commensurate with experience
START DATE: October 1993

United News Service is a relatively new radio network. We provide hourly updates and bottom of the hour headlines for nonprofit religious radio stations across the country. Currently we broadcast from studios in Washington, DC, and are interviewing for available positions for a new San Francisco bureau.

Send tape and resume to:

UNS NEWS, Attention: Personnel Director
450 Spear Street, Suite 200
San Francisco, CA 94111

The "religious" and nonprofit part spooked me. Buzz words for Bible thumpers and low pay. But I needed a new job. I had been doing traffic reports for the local news station the last year and I was bored. There are only so many ways to tell people that traffic sucks. I sent in my tape.

Two weeks later I got the call.

Two women interviewed me. Both were Christian, although that didn't come up. I sensed both needed a good going at. That didn't come up either. I had on my only suit, a gray thousand-dollar Italian job that I bought from my friend Marcel for a hundred bucks. Marcel worked at a Fillmore district parking lot I once managed between radio jobs. No retailers of fine men's clothing had been spared his penchant for thievery. Macy's. L'Uuomo. Ballerini's. Cielo. He'd even hit the Men's Wearhouse a time or two. After a productive night, the next day he'd show up at the lot, pop the trunk of his black BMW, and announce to the attendants, "Santee Kluz has arrived, boys!"

The interview went well. I'm always more at ease with women in these kind of situations and with all three of us sitting on the a plush sofa in the small lobby (there were no office chairs yet in the "San Francisco bureau") I felt cozy. Sharon and Amy double-teamed Marty. Sharon, who was to be my immediate supervisor, had long wavy blond hair, a soft face, and blue eyes. She stumbled on her words at the end of the interview when she asked me if I would have a problem doing news on religious radio. I told her I had no objections as long as I didn't have to praise the Lord after every newscast. Actually I was a bit less flip, but they got the message.

"Oh, no," said Amy. "We want seasoned and credible news people. We already have forty religious stations and we hope to get more. Eventually we'd like to sell the network to commercial stations of just about any format."

Sharon took it from there. "Of course we want to continue offering what our listeners want when it comes to news."

Here it comes. "What's that?"

"We try to stay away from sensationalism and we also like to do stories that are family oriented. . . ."

Great. I knew it! Spoon-feed the Christian Right. The funny thing was I half agreed with that news philosophy. Maybe because I needed the job, or maybe I'd had enough of covering multiple murders, sensational trials, crap about movie stars. I attempted to project myself as a serious journalist with integrity and high standards. If they hired me, I would gather and anchor the news in a separate news studio three blocks from the Family Broadcasting operations on Market Street. I would have to learn an audio computer program, which I figured I could handle. Finally, Sharon said they liked my tape and suggested that I listen to the San Francisco affiliate to get a feel for "our listeners." I'd worked for newstalk stations, public stations, country stations, rock stations and easy listening stations, but never had I been on a Christian station.

Let's see what I was getting myself into.

When I got home I tuned in KLVE, 107.1 FM. The first thing I heard was a man's voice that sounded South African. It was a calming, friendly voice.

. . . As the ground literally danced with earthquakes of unimaginable intensity, hills and mountains would have flowed like pudding. Is it possible that modern science has been blind to the evidences of such upheaval? A couple of generations ago geologists who believed in evolution saw no notable evidence of any great floods on earth. Gradually they began to conclude that much of our sedimentary rock is the result of great floods. More recently they have started to notice evidence that mountains can literally collapse and flow like pudding.

Some landslides are simple landslides where part of the mountain collapses. But sometimes the collapse turns into a flow that travels for many miles even across flat ground. Take for example the Blackhawk slide at the southern edge of the Mojave Desert. Here, massive marble fell one and half kilometers down and flowed another nine kilometers across the nearly flat desert. One description says that it looked as if the mountain simply turned into chocolate milk. Once scientists understood that this happens they began to recognize evidence that show this phenomenon is not unusual. As our scientific knowledge grows, the history recorded in the Bible becomes dramatically illustrated, not disproved.

Cue announcer:

Moments in Creation is a production of Bible Study Associates. For more information please write us at Family Broadcasting, San Francisco, California, 94133. Keep the Faith!

So I would be reporting news to fundamentalists. People who take the Bible literally. Idiots. Nice payback, Lord.

I took the job and signed a six-month contract with a six-month option.

It was the easiest news job I'd ever had.

I would get to work about 9 A.M., write four minutes of

news for a 10:00 newscast and three pages of headlines to last the entire day. After my first newscast I'd do phone interviews, check the wires over the Internet, monitor CNN and C-Span on the studio TV, check the audio feed from Washington, and write more news. By 11:30 I'd, for the most part, be done writing. Unless there was any late-breaking news, I'd slum until I left after my 2:30 headlines. My bosses left me alone and rarely visited the news studios. This gave me plenty of time to take short naps, walks to the shopping center across the street, or take an occasional sun bath at Justin Herman Plaza. I wasn't making tons of money, like others on the air in the market, but I had a certain freedom I'd never had before at work.

They never questioned my story selection and we weren't getting any nasty letters from the Bible-thumping listeners. Two months in I was cruising. They liked my work and the big boss, Tom Jordan, the friendly pot-bellied general manager, said they wanted to show their appreciation for some extra work I had done by taking me on a trip to Lake Tahoe. Tahoe? Uh-oh! This was it. They'd catch me off guard in the pristine Sierra and start soft-pedaling "Our Lord." I accepted. I never turn down free meals, free tickets, or free trips.

Friday, midday.

I was in the middle of writing a story about a proposed balanced budget amendment when the phone rang.

"UNS."

"What exactly does 'UNS' stand for?"

"Unlimited Nympho Service."

"Really? Do you provide the service or just farm out?"

"Farm out? Please! We have a capable staff of professional nymphomaniacs to fulfill your every deep, dark desire."

"Well, that's curious. I myself am a nymphomaniac. . .
Do you have any positions open?"

"Perhaps. But I have to warn you, we have very high
standards. Not just any sex-starved number can work for
UNS. You have to have certain qualities."

"Like what?"

"I'd rather not get into it over the phone, but if you're
interested we could set up an appointment for the written
portion of our nympho test."

"Nympho test? What kind of questions do you ask on
your *nympho* test?"

"The standard stuff; frequency of encounters, the number of current sexual partners, fetishes, techniques, any pet
names you have for your pussy."

"What do you need to know that for?"

"It's a screening deal. Are you interested, or what?"

"I don't know. What comes after the written test?"

"The oral test."

"Of course. Well, I'd have no trouble passing that."

"Really?"

"Who conducts the oral test?"

"You do. Uh. . . I do. I mean—"

"You mean, I suck your cock."

"Yes."

"Do you have a *big* cock?"

"Somewhat."

"Are you hard right now?"

"Not exactly."

"Not exactly?"

"Well, I'm getting—"

"What kind of pants do you have on?"

"Jeans."

"Do you have a belt on?"

"Yes."

"What color is it?"

"What?"

"What *color* is your belt?"

"Black."

"Good. Now unbutton your belt and undo your pants."

"Now?"

"Yes, now. . . Have you done what I told you?"

"Yes."

"Do you have on underwear?"

"No."

"Do you have an erection yet?"

"Yes."

"Very good. What hand are you holding the phone with?"

"My left."

"Now, I want you to, with your right hand take out your cock, but don't hold it. . . Have you done that?"

"Yes."

"Describe it."

"It's pointing up, and it's very hard."

"Are your balls tight?"

"Yes."

"Now, reach down with your right hand and gently finger the space between your asshole and your balls. . .

"Bring your hand up and cup your balls. . .

"Now slide your hand up and around your cock. . .

"Are you doing what I say?"

"Yes."

"Now, holding firm, but not too tight, stroke yourself. . . Slowly. Close your eyes and imagine a tongue licking at that place under your balls. Maybe my tongue. Maybe someone else's. Keep stroking. . .

"Slowly. . . Firmly, but don't come. There'll be time for that later. . .

"Now tell me, who's your sexy bitch?"

"You are."

"Do you want me?"

"Very much."

"You want my mouth on your hard cock?"

"More than you know."

"Do you worship my tongue?"

"Yes."

"Say it."

"I worship your tongue."

"Good. Now go back to work. I'll see you tonight."

I stood there with penis in hand in the studio where in less than six minutes I would be broadcasting the news to thousands of fundamentalists. Is this how Jim Bakker got his start?

There was no doubt. Sarah had me.

We were off to Sonoma that night. Forgetting that little scene with Paige at the Red Room, I was looking forward to a weekend of carnal indulgence and hoping that our phone encounter had been foreplay. But with Sarah you never knew. In an instant she could be as frigid as a summer night at Candlestick Park.

I wouldn't think about it.

CHAPTER 3

Seven-year-old Martin Fante had a dream.

He was in an enormous pit. Looking up beyond the dim light of small fires protruding from the rocky bottom all the boy could see was darkness, a darkness consumed in human sorrow. He was frightened, sensing a depth of suffering beyond his comprehension. He sat motionless on a wooden bench. He looked in the pit and through the flickering light he noticed other benches. They were lined with people all sitting in quiet torment. Marty turned his head and saw, across from him, his mother sitting on one of the benches. She was barefoot and dressed in a ripped T-shirt and tattered blue jeans. Her head was shaved and her hands were tied in front of her with thick white rope. She stared young Martin down with a wickedness so burning it made him turn away.

A group of men entered. They were all wearing leather with long dark hair tied back in ponytails. They motioned for Marty's mother to stand. She did, looking defiant, her eyes glassy, her lips parched and cracking. One of the men asked her two questions: *Do you believe in God?*

No.

Do you accept Satan as your master?

Yes.

As she was led away, upward into the blackness, she turned back and glared at Marty then began laughing. As her laugh echoed in the dark pit Martin awoke from the dream terrified and unable to fall back asleep.

It was sweltering in Southern California. Smog infiltrated the Valley like body odor on a homeless drunk, the sooty inversion shroud baking under an August sun. Any wind, even the warm Santa Ana's, would have been welcome relief.

It was a summer day. Freedom. Glorious independence from the world, from the night. For Marty and his best friend Michael Hammer, the daylight hours of summer were more than suspended time: they were the childhood joy of abandon.

During those days the tender-eyed Martin had one thing on his mind: the fort he and Mike were building at the old railroad depot near the Sepulveda dam. It would take them the better part of an hour to ride their sting rays to paradise: a ghost of a supply depot where the railroad tracks stretched to forever on the hot, dusty, unpaved road.

They'd found an old supply shack near the trestle and broke its rusty lock with a sledgehammer they discovered near the boxcar. Inside were metal buckets, pine panels, 2 by 4s, 2 by 12s, sagging makeshift shelves with rusted tools, which included a crescent wrench, broken pliers with blue plastic handle covers, and assorted screwdrivers. In the corner of the shed's dirt floor was a pair of mud-stiffened white gardener's gloves and a worn, tangled green rubber hose, minus the nozzle. The buckets were filled with nails of all sizes; big rusted ones, smaller dull-looking ones with flat heads, short ones with square heads. They had hit the Mother Lode! the treasure of all treasures! Without saying a word, both knew what was to be done: clear out the supply car and make a home.

They spent days organizing and separating their supplies to make things accessible for construction.

Occasionally an adult would wander by, but like the Indian scouts they imagined themselves to be, the two always heard the lumbering footsteps in advance of any sighting. They would hide in the shed until the enemy shuffling was at a safe distance.

Every morning they would meet at Mike's apartment. Four other kids slept in Michael's room, three brothers and a sister. Despite his lack of privacy, Mike was a loner. Marty liked to talk. Mike would listen, and work.

Michael would get out of bed before any of his siblings, just after his stepfather left for work at 6 A.M. He'd get dressed and wait for Marty outside, down the apartment stairs.

Marty lived with his mother six blocks away on Vanowen Street. She would leave to catch the 7:10 bus for downtown L.A., where she worked as a receptionist for a wholesale clothing manufacturer. Her good-bye kiss was his signal to wake up and wait for her to leave.

That particular morning the boys had planned to go scavenging for carpet. They hit every trash bin in the adult apartments along Vanowen. Adult buildings always had the best trash. They didn't find any carpet but they did discover some Alfred Hitchcock paperbacks, stacks of magazines including a *Sports Illustrated* with Wilt Chamberlain on the cover, and *Oui*, which they had never seen before. It quickly became their favorite.

They also found an old cast-iron skillet and a Ping-

Pong net and paddles. They didn't have any use for the skillet but Martin took it for his mother. They still had not suc-
ceeded in their primary goal for the day when Martin suggested they ride over to Carpeteria on Vallejo. Rummaging
through the dumpster, they hoped for some plush shag but
were satisfied when they found dozens of flat carpet scraps.
They put the square and rectangular pieces into plastic
trash bags they had emptied. They locked their bikes to a
sign post on Vallejo then headed toward the depot. They
trudged down Vallejo, up Vanowen, to Woodley, up
Sepulveda, until they reached the dam. When they got
there they unloaded then took a break.

Sitting in the boxcar with their feet dangling out its open
doors, Martin took the opportunity to bring up a subject the
boys had discussed early in their adventure.

"I brought my pocket knife."

"Where do you want to do it?"

"How about right here, now?"

"No. Where on our body?"

"Our wrists, where else?"

Marty took out his Swiss Army Knife and opened the
sharpest, longest blade. Michael was no chicken, but he was
intimidated by the prospect of having his wrist sliced open.
"Maybe we should just do our fingers, or our hands instead."

"Yeah, maybe we should just pick some scabs. . . . Don't
be a fucking pussy! If we want to be real blood brothers we
have to cut our *wrists*."

"How do you know?"

"I read it. That's the way the Apaches did it. They'd cut
their wrists then shake hands like Blacks. You know like
brothers. They took a vow to protect each other until death.
Geronimo was an Apache. He had magic powers—medicine—after the Mexicans killed his family. He couldn't be
killed by any white man's bullet."

They looked at each other with a stern determination, then Martin said, "I'll do *both* wrists."

He took from his pocket a roll of surgical tape and some gauze he had stolen from the pharmacy near his apartment. He put them down between his legs. He picked up the knife, blade extended, and with his left hand brought it to his right wrist. He squeezed the right palm into a fist and sliced at just the right depth to produce an oozing of blood. He pinched back a cunning, burning pain.

Before his arm drowned in blood, he reached over as Michael watched in horrified wonder and did the same to his wrist. They leaned down and put their elbows on the car's planked floor. Marty declared, "forever blood brothers," and the boys embraced palms, rubbing together their wrists and forearms. They wiped the blood off with some carpet scraps, put the gauze on the wounds, and wrapped the white tape around their wrists up over their thumbs.

Then they worked. They nailed down the carpet, arranged the books and other stuff they had found in the garbage, and put all the carpet scraps into the trash bag. They hung up their posters, then sat down and looked at naked ladies in their new magazines. Occasionally they changed the dressings on their arms when they were soaked with blood.

Martin had lost all track of time and arrived home after dark. He went through the back door and sneaked into his bedroom.

The room was in shambles. His single bed had been dragged off its frame, the bedspread and sheets crumpled on the floor. His posters had been ripped off the wall and shredded. His closet door was open and his white plastic quilted toy box overturned in the middle of the floor.

All his toys were strewn throughout the room: his Hot

Wheels set, his black baseball bat, his etch-a-sketch, his baseball cards, his Wilson football that his uncle Dominic had given him for Christmas, his Dodger batting helmet that he got during helmet weekend at Dodger Stadium, his microscope, his mini drum set. All were scattered on the green carpet.

Marty's body recoiled. Part of him went vacant. Another part screamed *run!* But it was useless. Suddenly his mother hovered over him, her eyes blazing. "Who the fuck do you think you are coming home at this hour?"

Martin had no answer.

She backhanded him across the face. "Answer me, you little bastard!"

"I don't know," the boy whispered.

"You don't know?" she screamed as she grabbed a wooden drumstick for the floor and lunged toward him. "Do you know that I was worried sick?"

Martin scurried to a nearby wall then shrank to the floor. "Please, Mom."

"Please what, fucker!" And she pummeled him with the drumstick. With the full force of her fury she beat his small arms, his back, his legs, his rear. Over and over he felt the sting, then the burn of her blows. "I'm the mother, you're the child! You do what I tell you. Do you understand? I'm the mother. You do what your mother tells you!"

He put his head beneath his arms. He was disappearing and in a moment he would feel nothing. But until then there was just the pain. The bashing pain. The disabling pain. The total pain. The dying pain.

As he started to drift she let go a yell as if not to be denied. "Ahhh. . . !"

She stampeded out the doorway and chucked the drumstick against the boy's crumpled body. He jerked as the thick end hit his bare leg.

Martin remained still for minutes before getting up. He wiped the tears from his face with his shirt sleeve. He put the bed back on its frame, making it, and then cleaned up his room. He lay down on the mattress. With every subtle movement he felt the residual sting of his mother's blows. He remained motionless, his mind clear and his feelings escaping like a vapor out his ears and eyes.

About an hour later there was a soft knock on the door. "Marty? Marty? Can I come in?"

"Come in."

Her hair was messed, her mascara was running, her eyes were soggy and bloated. She inched toward the bed. Martin didn't move. She crawled up close and took him in her arms. She began sobbing. "I'm sorry, Marty. I'm so sorry. Please forgive me Marty. Your mother loves you, Marty. She loves you more than anything on earth. My beautiful boy. I'm so sorry."

When she finally left, Martin walked into his closet, closed the door, and lay down on his toy box. He fell asleep and dreamed of his fort.

CHAPTER 4

Sonoma suits Sarah perfectly. Its maze of dusty roads that lead to the more obscure of the region's wineries are as perplexing as her emotions. And like her feelings, just when you think you've got it down, you get lost all over again. The town square is inviting with its four streets lined with shops, restaurants, quaint art galleries, and one movie theater tucked in among small open engraved, wooden doors and hand-painted signboards. Walking the streets you can easily lose all sense of direction. But once out of the town's central plaza each street leads to its own separate world: the vineyards, the freeway, the neighborhoods, the river.

We drove up Mission Street. Sarah's bootleg Velvet Underground tape was playing. I glanced toward her. She was looking out her window grooving to "I Can't Stand it."

As we passed the Sonoma Mission my thoughts turned toward the simply built structure and what life must have been like back then. Recently the Catholic Church's effort to beatify Father Junipero Serra had been in the news. The

Franciscan Friar had almost single handedly transformed California from a heathen haven of unruly and uncivilized savage natives to a land filled with God-fearing converts. The Mission system lasted only forty years, before the Mexicans seized control of the territory from Spain in 1821, but Junipero's influence remains unquestioned. Catholic scholars however have yet to document evidence that he performed a miracle which has held up his official sainthood. At least he had a freeway named after him. How many priests can claim that?

The first sunny weekend in some time brought a vibrant color and light to the valley that grabbed hold of my senses. The sunshine dispersed through the sparse pine trees and caressed the green hills. Acres upon acres of vineyards emitted a dull, sweet fragrance. Grapes for the gods, heaven for the angels descending upon the restless ghosts of the Pomo, Patwin, Wappo, and Miwok tribes, the Spanish settlers and the Mexican soldiers, the white American artists fleeing from civilization.

We pulled over and got out of the car. A soft breeze blew some dirt my way. Ah, the dirt! It felt like baptism, like Guerrero Negro, like San Fernando Valley lemon orchards, like taking ground balls off my father's bat, like Cochise in Pa-Gotzin-Kay, like adolescence, like Jesus in Galilee, like dawn, like the Sepulveda dam.

Would the dirt heal the wounds that Sarah and I had inflicted on each other?

Sarah was in high spirits. She was a different person outside the city, more agreeable, more harmonious. She smiled at me and asked, "Have you ever stayed at the Sonoma Inn?"

"Never."

"I think you'd like it."

"Why?"

"Every room has a fireplace or wood-burning stove. . . ."

antiques, hardwood floors, brass bedposts, bookshelves filled with classics. . . ."

"Sounds charming." I resisted asking her who she'd been there with.

"You want to take a look? It's just down the block."

The desk clerk was a handsome middle-aged woman with cropped hair and warm smile. Sarah did all the talking and asked the clerk how many rooms were available and if we could take a look before making a decision.

The woman handed us four keys and offered to show us each room. Sarah declined. Without hesitation, the woman gave us a floor map of the rooms and a list of prices.

The first and only room we checked out was halfway down the hall on the second floor. As we walked in Sarah closed the door behind us while we quickly surveyed our surroundings. The room felt homey. It had a fireplace in the corner. Its bay windows overlooked the town square and its queen sized bed was covered with a hand woven, beige, burgundy, and dark blue bed spread. Sarah looked down at it, then turned her lascivious eyes on me. Even before she slipped her tongue under my upper lip I was hard. I turned her around and put her hands on the mattress. She spread her legs and arched her ass up as she inched her feet out from the bed. I lifted up her printed earth-toned sun dress and pulled her panties down and off.

And then I was fucking her.

My legs began to tremble as the warmth of her cunt grabbed then pulled me deeper inside. My balls tickled against her asshole as I pushed up further and further until I felt her cervix. I had to think to breathe. All my vitals seemed to be escaping up into her body through my cock: my respiration, my heartbeat, my thermostat.

As I took in a deep, long breath, she tilted her head back and moaned. I leaned over and kissed her open mouth. But I would still wait to come. I closed my eyes and

stood there, deep inside her, without moving. As my heartbeat began to slow we uncoupled. I buttoned my jeans. I
helped steady Sarah as she stood up. We embraced. Then I
picked up her panties from the floor and put them in my
coat pocket.

We left the room, both of us flush and feeling as if the
breeze could lift us up beyond the dense, sunlight saturated
green hills.

Our weekend in Sonoma was an edgy, suspended bliss.
Sarah talked me into spending an extra night and calling in
sick for Monday. I phoned Sharon and told her I must have
caught something over the weekend and we would have to
postpone our lunch date. She wished me well. It was the
first time I'd called in sick and I felt guilty, but that quickly passed as Sarah reached across and pulled me close. We
lay in bed and spoke of our first trip together. We had just
met when I asked her to go away. We had driven to Nevada
City and stayed at the National Hotel, famous for housing
Mark Twain when he lived in nearby Virginia City.

We reminisced about how we went fishing and panning
for gold on the Yuba river and how I tied her to the bed post
and tortured her with a peacock feather before taking my
pleasure. Now, despite our physical closeness, I couldn't
shake the feeling that she was distancing herself. I pretended not to notice the little things that tipped her hand; her
lack of eye contact, her refusal to talk about any future
plans, her spending more time with Paige. I was being over-
sensitive. *Don't be too available.* I was crazy to think that I
could capture Sarah and make her wholly mine. Her inac-
cessibility fueled my obsession. The more sex we had the
more I needed her near. I'd remained aloof with women my
entire life, but Sarah's luscious indifference made me care.
And now this weekend. She was dangerous and fragile. As

she refused to lose herself in me, I felt compelled to continue the chase.

On the drive home I was talkative and in good spirits. But Sarah drifted. I asked what was wrong. "Nothing." I let it be and took in the scenery as we drove along Highway 37 then down 101. As we headed out of the Waldo tunnel and approached the Golden Gate Bridge with San Francisco sparkling in the distance I remarked how lucky we were to live in such a beautiful and enchanted city. Sarah stared at me with contempt, then turned and looked out the window toward the ocean. Back at my apartment she said I had a way of ruining things by stating the obvious.

"Saying something is beautiful doesn't make it any less beautiful."

"You talk too much." Her venom sinking into my bones. "And now of course you don't have anything to say."

"It was a great weekend. I'm not going to let you ruin it."

"You don't understand anything do you?"

"What is it I don't understand Sarah. Why don't *you* tell me? Why don't you explain it?"

"I can't stand being in this apartment right now. I'm leaving."

"Where are you going?"

"None of your fucking business. Get off me!"

And she left.

CHAPTER 5

Someteos pues a dios: resitid al diablo, y vosotros huira.

Allegaos a dios, y el se allegara a vosotros. Pecadores, limpiad las manos; y vosotros de doblando animo, purifcad los corazones.

Afligios y lamentad, y llorad. Vuestros gozo en tristeza.

Humillaos selante del Senor, y el os ensalzara.

. . . Speak not evil of one another, brethren. He that speaketh evil of his brother, and judgeth his brother, speaketh evil of the law: but if thou judge the law, thou art not a doer of law, but a judge.

James 4:11

"When are you going to learn Spanish, mijo?"

"I know Spanish, grandma. Como esta usted, abuelita?"

"Muy bien, mijito. Aye! You'll learn someday. It's okay."

Elena Castillo was eighty-seven years old. Her eyesight and her hearing were just about shot, but her mind was still sharp. Recently I'd been calling her a lot, at least once a week. She lived in Fullerton and I rarely got down to visit. She was a devout Baptist. A Mexican Baptist. A rarity.

"Have you been going to church, Marty?"

"Not in awhile, grandma."

"Go to church, Marty. It's important. Do you read the Bible I gave you?"

"Sometimes."

"You used to be so cute. You knew your Bible so well when you were little. You used to tell me all the books of the Old and New Testament in order. Remember?"

"I remember."

I had been raised Baptist by my heathen parents. Both my mother and my father had turned their backs on the Church. My Catholic father ignored his altar boy upbringing after my uncle Freddy was excommunicated for marrying a statuesque, European divorcee who had fled Nazi Germany. My mother despised the Church on overall principle. She wasn't going to be subjected to the judgments of a sexist, old man somewhere in the sky.

Nonetheless, from kindergarten to the fourth grade I attended a private Baptist elementary school: Valley Christian School. For academic purposes, my parents said. Once, when I came home from kindergarten at our local public school, they asked what I had learned that day. I didn't have much to say except we took a nap and had recess. My mother had taught me to read almost as soon as I began talking and she continued reading to me almost every night through my childhood. She thought I was beyond the ABCs and See Spot Runs that I was getting at school, so she yanked me and put me in Valley Christian. I don't think my parents were aware of the religious discipline and steady dose of fire and brimstone I'd get. Every morning we went to services at the school's small sanctuary, where Pastor Reeves would flail and spit, and bellow the Word of God. According to the Pastor, who was also the school principal, God was a loving god, but don't fuck with him and his rules—or the pain you would suffer would make any earthly hardship seem like a trip to Disneyland. Okay, Reverend, no need to tell me more than once. But he told us everyday.

In the classroom we spent as much time memorizing and interpreting the Bible as we did on our geography and multiplication tables. My impressionable mind accepted the "facts" that the Jews were condemned for not accepting Jesus as the Messiah and that it was my duty to convert all those in my universe into loving Jesus, else I would be damned to an eternity of Hellfire.

When my parents divorced I continued at Valley Christian for just half of the fifth grade. It was 1969 and I was becoming a young hippie. My hair was long and I wore love beads and sunglasses I thought looked like John Lennon's granny glasses. I was told at school to cut my hair and lose the beads. I told my mother, who by that time was thinking of moving us to a commune in Humboldt County. We stood our ground and finally I was suspended. The next day she walked me down to Bassett Street Elementary School. My nonsecular education was over. The only time I went to church after that was when I spent time with my mother's mother.

Our conversations then centered on the aftermath of my grandfather's death.

"You know Marty, your mother had a very difficult time after your grandfather died."

"So I've heard."

"Your uncle Pauly was a hard child and, I think, took your grandfather's death out on your mother."

"I know. She's still mad about it. She won't talk to him."

"Your uncle's not so bad, Marty. No one understands him like I do. He's scared of things, you know."

"He still scares my mother."

"I wish she could forgive him. I wish my children loved each other."

"Did grandpa beat Paul a lot?"

"Pablito was bad sometimes. He started getting mean and your grandfather had to discipline him. I've never talked about it, mijito, but your uncle still feels bad."

"For what?"

"When grandpa was sick he told me, 'I hope he dies.'"

Pablo Castillo had died of lung cancer fifteen years before I was born. I was told he had transformed the Baptist Church in California while he and my grandmother raised a family. When he got sick, the family tried everything they could to save him. They brought in a Christian faith healer and a *curandera*, as well as the usual team of doctors. He died six months after being diagnosed. My mother had been his favorite. She would talk of him with a pain that never escaped her. "The others hated me because your grandfather adored me. He never laid a hand on me, but he used to beat the shit out of your uncle Paul. But the demon child got even once my father died."

My grandmother was left to raise four children on a missionary's meager pension and a few Social Security dollars. She was tight-lipped about the time she spent with her husband. She never remarried.

As she grew older the pain of the past turned to nostalgia and she had a curious audience in me.

"Back in Texas your grandfather was so handsome."

"When did you meet him?"

"In 1929. In El Paso. Your grandfather had just moved from Guanajuanto to attend the seminary. We were both

Catholic back then. It was before we were married." My grandmother, whose mother was of Mimbreno Apache tribe and whose father was of Spanish and Irish descent, had lived her entire life in Texas. She told me how she would see my grandfather in the small church at the edge of town, how he would stare at her while she sat with her parents and sisters. Pictures of the teenaged Elena showed her to be small and delicate, with an understated sensuality. Her *nogal*-colored eyes and long, dark brown hair, which she wore tied in a loose bun, must have taken hold of my grandfather's senses.

When I was a child, my grandmother had showed me books of photos from El Paso. The town's people back then were mostly Mexicans who had not gotten used to the idea that they lived in the United States. They felt the U.S. stole Texas. Chickens, cattle, small brick and wooden homes dotted the dirt countryside. She and my grandfather would meet for lunch and talk about the scriptures.

My grandmother was consumed by Pablo's breadth of knowledge concerning the Bible "He knew all the scriptures, always quoting the writings of *Santiago, San Juan, San Lucas,* and *San Mateo. Y encantador!* Thick black hair combed back under his white Fedora. Round, brown eyes, full of fire but at the same time soft, forgiving. His teeth were white and strong, his skin brown as Texas soil. He was not a very big man, like you, but walked tall. I knew he would become a great minister."

He never touched her until they moved to California.

One day during lunch together, she noticed a change. Pablo seemed preoccupied, somber. She asked if anything was troubling him. He said that when he was younger and lived in Mexico, he had relations with an older woman, who became pregnant. She planned to move to Los

Angeles and live with an aunt. Her child would be born a U.S. citizen and she would learn English and become an American as well. My grandfather wouldn't hear of it. He demanded that they be married and remain in their village. She said that she was moving to California and nothing was going to stop her. He would not allow her to leave.

They were secretly married the next day by the priest who had baptized Pablo.

One night shortly after that she sneaked away and moved to the San Fernando Valley in Los Angeles, where she lived with an aunt and picked oranges for a living.

My grandfather relocated to El Paso and enrolled in the seminary where he met my grandmother. His wife gave birth to a daughter, Rosa. She heard that Pablo was in Texas and sent him a picture of their child.

After Pablo had been at the seminary for a year, the priest in Mexico who married the couple had learned that he was planning on becoming a man of the cloth. The priest loved my grandfather but could not allow such a sacrilege to occur. He told the Church.

The would-be priest was excommunicated.

My grandmother stuck with him. She loved him and he had a plan. He was a man of God and nothing was going to stop him from completing his quest. It was then he asked her to marry him.

They moved to California where Pablo found work as a cook in an Italian restaurant while waiting to be accepted to the Baptist seminary. "Your grandfather made many mistakes in his life, but I loved him and admired his will. He was blessed with the faith of a saint and I needed to be with him. His eyes were so tender and. . . powerful. Of all the grandchildren, you're the only one who has those eyes, Marty."

My grandmother and I would talk on the phone for hours. She told me of their years in Los Angeles, how it was hard at first with my grandfather's dark skin and obvious Mexican features. It was a decade before the zoot suit riots and racial tensions were at a zenith. There were signs in some establishments: *No Mexicans allowed.* One night while walking home from work my grandfather was beaten by a group of white sailors.

"Why don't you go back to Mexico, spic!" *Whack!*

"Yeah, greaser. Why don't you go back to the farm! You and your wetback friends are taking jobs away from Americans." *Smack!*

My grandmother got a job as a seamstress, making five cents a piece. Both kept their dignity until Pablo was accepted to the seminary.

He shined. It was evident to the Church leaders that he would make a fine minister. Soon after he was ordained he was given a small Mexican parish in Boyle Heights. Initially very few people came to services, but Pablo made many friends in the neighborhood. Word got out about the charismatic Baptist minister and soon the pews were filled.

The Church, which had provided the young couple with a small house near their congregation, had taken notice. They realized that there was an untapped market: the Mexicans. They decided to make Pablo Castillo a missionary.

Traveling from community to community, he would set up local parishes, increase the congregation, then move on. There would always be a transition period while a new bilingual minister was trained. The Church provided the Castillos with a trailer truck and sent them on their way. First stop: San Fernando.

It made Pablo happy to be in the Valley. He could see his daughter, who he visited often. His daughter and his first wife became part of the congregation. My grandmother never complained.

Back then the Valley was the country. It was before strip malls, before boulevards, before fast food and freeway overpasses. There was more dirt than concrete with miles of orange groves and open fields. They stayed in the Valley three years. It was 1933 when they left there. Elena was twenty-four years old then.

They spent a year or so in Ventura, Santa Barbara, San Luis Obispo, Atascadero before they settled in Lompoc, the town where Pablo Castillo would die. They had four children along the way. The eldest, my uncle Paul, was born in San Fernando. My mother took her first breath during their year in Santa Barbara. The two youngest, my uncle Rueben and my aunt Martha, were born in Lompoc.

Trumpets blew and drums bellowed. A crowd had gathered along 3rd Street for the parade. The reverend Pablo Castillo had all four children with him, all impatient for the horses, and the marching band, and the soldiers. "Papa, I can hear them They're coming! They're coming!" Little Laurita was sitting on her father's shoulders.

"Si, mijita. They're on their way."

Pablito, standing at his father's side, asked, "Papa, will the soldiers have guns?"

"Callate, hijo! You'll see once they get here."

"But—"

"Callate!"

The children had never witnessed such pomp. Dressed in school colors of blue and gold, the Lompoc High School marching band paraded in step with the rhythm of the drumbeat. A company of the 3rd infantry had made the trek from Monterey. A division rode by proud and lithe. It was the 4th of July.

Laura, Martha, and Rueben all watched as if in a trance. Pablito, however, was overwhelmed. He was too excited to just stand there and watch. As the soldiers marched by he bolted toward the second row.

"Pablito!" His father shouted. he set down Laura and ran after his oldest son. The crowd gasped as the young boy tripped over the boot heel of one of the soldiers, none of whom broke ranks. In one swift move the reverend grabbed Pablito under his arm and whisked him back to where the other children were watching. They were used to their brother's antics.

"Are you crazy, boy? Tienes loco?" His father glared at Pablito and told him not to move. He then picked up Laurita, gave her a kiss, and hoisted her back on to his shoulders. When they arrived home Elena was busy in the kitchen making flour tortillas. She asked how the parade was. Her husband told her it was fine but that Pablito had ruined it for everyone. He'd have to be punished. Elena shook her head as she patted an uncooked tortilla.

The reverend took his son out back and whipped him. He beat Pablito with the belt he used to hold up his jeans, a thick black belt with a cowboy-engraved metal buckle. The reverend held the boy down with one arm and beat him with the other. Pablito got loose and began running. His father chased after him. He began swinging at the eight-year-old striking him across the back and legs as he ran. Finally Pablito fell to the ground. His father continued flailing, not stopping until he was winded. The entire episode occurred in a vacuum of silence. Both Pablos said nothing. No screams, no crying, no harsh words.

After the beating the reverend went inside and ate dinner.

Pablito swallowed his tears, walked into the house, washed his face in the bathroom, then sat down and ate with the other children. He looked at his mother with heavy eyes. She handed him a plate of beans and fideo and shook her head. "Pablito, Pablito."

No one had witnessed the beating, except Laura. She had no fear of her father. She had watched out the bedroom window.

CHAPTER 6

"Sir. Excuse me, sir? Have you accepted Jesus Christ as your Lord and Savior?"

"I don't have time for this. Sorry, I'm late for work."

"That's a shame. Everyone should have time for our Lord and Savior."

"*Your* Lord and Savior. I'm Hindu. Vishnu said, 'There are many paths to righteousness.'" (Maybe it was Rama, or Krishna who said that).

"If you were to accept Jesus into your heart maybe you would feel differently."

"Wait a minute! Are you a Jehovah's Witness or a Mormon?"

"I'm with the Church of Latter-Day Saints, sir."

"So you're a Mormon. Why in the hell do you people insist on shoving your beliefs down other people's throats?"

"The Bible says—"

"The Bible says to be tolerant and accepting."

"We are tolerant and accepting. We just want to share

the glorious, wonderful truth of our Savior."

"That's the point! You want to manipulate and force your 'truth' on others!"

"No, sir, we—"

"'No sir,' your dick! What the fuck are you doing then?"

"I—"

"You're selling your religion so that your so-called Church can make more money and have more influence. . . politically, financially, morally! You're the scourge of the day! The Nazis, the Sovietism, the Inquisition of our time!"

"That's not true, sir."

"And if you don't believe that, you're being duped. Used. You're a whore. A Jesus whore!"

"Thank you, sir. Have a nice day."

"Have a nice day? Have a nice day! Yeah, well fuck you too, pal. Hey! Where are you going? Gets a little tough and you turn tail! What kind of soldier for the Lord are you? Hey! Come back here, Jesus whore! Come back and tell me why I should believe *your* truth? That's right! Get the fuck out of here!"

So I was a little harsh with the Mormon. I had a lot on my mind. It was my first day back to work after the Sonoma trip and I was running late. I had 9:30 headlines and it was 9:10. I'd just parked my motorcycle and was rushing past Embarcadero 1 when Brigham Young caught me off guard. I felt bad for a millisecond, then filed it under *urban street hazards*.

When I got to work there was a message on my voice mail from Sharon. "Are we still on for lunch?" I called her and left a message to me meet after my noon cast at the Silver Cloud. The place was always crawling with suits and the service was bad, but it was close to work, and had an outdoor dining area along the water. It would be nice.

I checked the wires and the fax machine. There was the usual propaganda: a Christian Coalition news release condemning the president's veto of a bill that would have outlawed partial birth abortions and a release from the Alliance Defense League urging us all to pray that federal judges make the right decision concerning a number of cuts from those opposed to the president's veto.

One particular bite from a Republican congressman from Orange County, who always struck me as a fascist lunatic, compared the veto to Nazi directives to implement the Final Solution. I used his comments, but I also called the director of a local abortion clinic.

Sharon didn't mention any of my newscasts at lunch, so I assumed she didn't tune in. Whenever she listened she usually said something, if only "sounding good." We sat outside in the back patio of the restaurant.

"How are things in the newsroom? Everything working okay?"

"Pretty much. It still takes forever to get online. Also we need some paper for the printer."

"We're working to get DSL, so soon you won't have to dial-up. Tom is comparison shopping. Looks like we're going to go with AT&T. We should have that by the end of next week. And I'll tell Tom to drop off some paper later today."

"Great."

Then she brought up the Tahoe trip. "If you can be at the office early Saturday morning, about 8:00, we could get an early start."

"So I'll be driving with you?"

"Me, Steve, and the boys."

"Sure, no problem."

"How was your weekend with Sarah?"

I was apprehensive about discussing my private life with my born-again boss, but she seemed genuinely interested, so I unloaded. "I don't know. I'm just not sure with Sarah. One minute we're fine then the next we're at each other's throats. It wouldn't be so bad if I wasn't so into her. We could split up and be friends. But it's so intense, like it's all or nothing with us, and I want everything."

It was more than I wanted to say and I felt uneasy but Sharon pressed on and I found myself opening up.

"What do you fight about?"

"We have different philosophies on everything."

"And that makes you fight?"

"It makes her tune me out, which upsets me. When I try to discuss our differences she zones out. She can turn cold in an instant. When she does start to open up a bit she goes on the attack. . . and there are other things."

"Like what?"

". . . So are we going to ski in Tahoe?"

"You don't want to talk about it. That's fine. It's just that I think maybe she doesn't know how good she has it with you."

"Oh, yeah? Thanks, Sharon, but, you hardly know me."

"Well, it's just a feeling I have. What are the 'other things'?"

"She makes it pretty clear she doesn't respect what I do for a living. She thinks I'm wasting away, that I should be doing something more creative. Paint or write or act. Something that has more artistic integrity than report on other people. It's funny. She can see the poetry in a construction worker paving the road, but what I do is a 'facade.' You believe that? When I ask her what she's doing with such a loser she laughs and says she adores me. Ha!"

"Do you think maybe it's a sex thing?"

"Maybe. The sex is great, there's no doubt about it. But

even that's starting to fade. It's like she needs the intellectual connection to sustain it. When it's not there we still do it, hoping the primal part will get us there somehow. But she won't let it. I don't know. It's frustrating."

"She sounds confused."

"We're both unsure. How long have you and Steve been married?"

"Eighteen years."

"How have you done it?"

"It hasn't been easy, that's for sure. Sometimes I can't believe it myself. Steve and I are very different.

"He can sometimes be impatient. I have too much energy for him, so he says. I think we've settled into a sort of understanding, a compromise, a friendship that works. The boys keep us tied together. Not in a bad way. We both enjoy them very much, seeing them grow and change. But there's not much excitement in our marriage. Sad to say but true."

"Eighteen years is a long time. I don't know if it's possible to keep things hot that long."

She looked away. "My faith keeps me strong. I know that God has His plans and I'm just doing my best to live accordingly."

It took the usual four hours to get to Lake Tahoe's south shore. I rode up front with Sharon's husband. He smiled a lot but didn't talk much. Sharon and the couple's two boys were in the back eager to make the road trip fun. The boys, Jack who was in his late teens, and Donny, about twelve or thirteen, had heard me on the radio a few times. They were curious about me and picked my brain on everything from U.S. history to the Beatles. About a half hour into the trip all but Sharon's husband Steve were loose and having a good time. He seemed preoccupied with the details of the trip: the best route to take, where to stop and eat, the gray clouds in the distance. He asked Sharon if Tom had paid for the rooms yet.

We arrived at the Hyatt about 2 P.M., checked in, and agreed to meet up an hour later. I had my own room and Sharon's family had one. Tom and his wife, Janet, a round woman with short brown hair and an intelligent face, had arrived a day earlier. We all met up in the casino. All, except Janet, were up for some gaming.

Tom and Steve were a bit timid at first but eventually they jumped in. Sharon attacked the table with the zeal of a vote-hungry politician. Tom and Sharon had their own show at the radio station: *Missionaries for Peace*. I had no doubt that they were fundamentalists. I was surprised at their tolerance—in Sharon's case, enthusiasm—for gambling. I thought that was something the Assemblies of God-Pat Robertson-Christian Coalition crowd would abhor. Hadn't I heard something about temptation and preying off the weak?

Sharon, who looked seductive in a low-cut purple chiffon dress, was obviously intimate with the nuances of blackjack. We sat at a single-deck, five dollar table. She played third base by the book, hitting when called for and staying when the dealer showed a six or less. She took chances though, doubling down whenever she had the opportunity, increasing her bet when she felt lucky. She split nines once when the dealer was showing an eight. The dealer busted. She was a ballsy player.

However after nearly an hour at the table she was down about fifty dollars. I was down ten. She was drinking screwdrivers one after the other but she didn't appear drunk. Tom and Steve left the table about a half hour in, saying they'd meet us for dinner in the buffet. We told them we'd meet at 6:00. I had to drag Sharon from the table. "One more hand," she said a dozen times.

Sharon was antsy throughout dinner. I'd seen that look

in friends, obsessive friends. In Vegas Joe Primesberger had once stayed at the table seven straight hours. He ended up losing twelve hundred dollars. We were twenty-one and couldn't afford to lose a hundred, let alone twelve. He maxed out his student credit card getting cash advances at $3.50 a pop. The casinos don't care if you're playing with rent money. They just keep the drinks coming.

We had wine with dinner. I kept my buzz and Sharon matched me glass for glass. She was sitting between me and her older kid. As she was relating a story about an interview she'd conducted with an Indianapolis missionary, she put her hand on my knee. At that exact moment the waiter brought over the coffee. Sharon leaned over and whispered in my ear, "I can't wait to get back to the tables."

I agreed.

Dinner dragged on with everyone sharing missionary adventures. I occasionally chimed in with an opinion about one news story or another.

Then we were at the craps table.

Sharon had rolled craps before, but she played it cool, asking questions as a surrogate for her husband, who seemed only half interested. Tom got into it. At first all he played was the pass line, but then he got nervy and started throwing out five dollar chips on to the field. We got hot. Sharon hit her point four times in a row and I rolled my number three straight. Everyone at the table was happy. Then Steve left to play blackjack. We continued, holding our own, but Tom started losing when no one rolled the field for a stretch. Finally he said that he'd had enough and left for his room. Sharon let out a sigh as if someone had just lifted a hundred pound pack off her back. She looked at me with a glimmer and said, "Your roll, Marty."

I chose my dice and told her to ask God for a seven. She laughed. I rolled an eight. The players, including Sharon, were barking out commands to the dealer. "Hard eight for twenty, five on the field, twenty on the come. . ." She already had twenty on the pass line. With odds, she could score a nice bundle if I hit. I backed up my bet and flicked the dice. Six rolls later, two fours came up: eight the hard way. The players at the table went wild. Sharon jumped up and yelled, then kissed my cheek. My next roll I hit seven. I was hot. I hit my point three times before I crapped out. The players were grateful and enthusiastic.

One guy threw me a fifty dollar chip. Sharon had been playing fifty and twenty dollar chips. She had a thick stack when the dealer passed her the dice. She rolled three straight sevens. We owned that table. I was up five hundred dollars. Sharon's stack totaled about a thousand. Finally we went cold. We started giving our money back. I'd gone this route too many times so I grabbed Sharon's arm and said, "Let's take a break."

"Marty, we're hot!"

"Not any more. Come on, just a minute to catch our breath."

"Okay, you're the boss. No, I'm the boss, and I say we stay right here!"

"I don't think so. Come on."

"Whatever you say, stud puppy!"

Stud puppy? She was as loose as a David Byrne suit. I looked at my watch. It was 2:30. We had planned, with the entire crew, to go skiing the next morning. I mentioned to Sharon that it was late and that we should probably go to bed. As she stumbled from the table she frowned and said, "I suppose you're right." But as quickly as the lights had dimmed, I saw a flash in her eyes that synchronized to the ringing bells on a nearby slot. She had a brilliant idea and was about to share. "Let's go to the hot tub!"

"What?"

"There's a hot tub downstairs. Our room keys will get us in."

A hot tub sounded good. Should I chance it? "I don't know, Sharon. It's late and we have to get up early."

"Oh, come on! Are you tired? I'm kind of pumped up. Doesn't a hot tub sound good?"

"You win. I'm going to run to my room and get my suit. I'll meet you there in five minutes."

The hot tub was perfect. The temperature was just right; for some reason it always is when you're in the mountains in winter. Sharon was already in when I got down. She was naked. I decided not to make it an issue. The bubbles and the dim lights made it easy for me to pretend I didn't notice. But I couldn't help observe her trying not to look at me as I quickly got into the hot tub.

"Does it bother you that I don't have any clothes on?"

"I hadn't really noticed."

"I didn't want to wake Steve and the boys, so I came straight down."

Her hair was wet and slicked back. It looked darker than usual. Her face was covered with a thin shroud of perspiration. I looked away and commented, "Boy, we really got hot, didn't we?"

"What?"

"On the table."

"Oh, yeah. I love gambling, especially when I'm winning."

A good opportunity for me to bring her back to her Christian sensibilities. "I thought gambling was a sin?"

"You have a lot of misconceptions about us born-agains, don't you, Marty?"

"I just thought—"

"No, it's okay. Most people do. We're not Mormons you know."

"Just what denomination are you?"

"We're with the Assemblies of God Church. Evangelical. Which unfortunately gets a bad rap."

"Jim Bakker, Jimmy Swaggart, Aimee McPherson. They were all evangelical. Not exactly poster children for integrity."

"Sure, there's been some charlatans posing as agents of the Lord, but like with every profession, there are bad apples. We believe that Jesus is the one true savior and we live our lives according to what he said and how he lived. But we're not perfect like *He* was. We try but we understand that Jesus knows we sometimes slip. I like to drink occasionally.

"I rarely gamble, but when I do, I enjoy it. And I have to tell you, Marty, like any woman. . ." She stood up and started toward me, "I like sex."

"I don't think this a good idea."

"Do you find me attractive, Marty?" She was standing nude not three feet away.

"You're married, Sharon. And you're my boss for God's sake."

She put her arms around me. Her white breasts pressed against my chest. Before kissing me she whispered in my ear, "For God's sake, Marty. For *God's sake*." The steam from the hot tub drifted up around our prone bodies. She walked me over to the hot tub steps and took off my trunks. She sat me down, then climbed onto the step my feet rested on, straddling my waist. She reached down between her legs and guided my hardness toward her vagina. The hot water had dried the outside of her opening so I squeezed my rear muscles and pushed. She gave a throaty gasp. Halfway in I started to glide. She sat down as far as she could, grinding into me as she gripped my chest. Then she pushed up on her toes, at first slowly then gradually picking up momentum. The water began splashing over the sides of the hot tub. As her rhythm quickened I noticed she was laboring. I reached down and held her pumping behind with both hands, helping to steady her.

As she bounced atop me, keeping time with my thrusts, she grasped my hair and leaned her head down, and began sucking my mouth and ears. "Oh, God," she said in husky voice. "Oh, God, Marty."

Her desperate lovemaking made my surrender that much easier.

When I woke I immediately called my apartment. I hoped that Sarah would answer. I had to talk to her, to tell her I loved her and missed her and everything could work out between us if we tried. All we needed was to try, because no romance is perfect. But if we pledged our love and vowed to communicate, it could work. If we agreed that we were different, that we had different needs, we could love each other in spite of our separate torments.

After two rings the answering service clicked on. My voice. It repelled me. What was I covering up? Who was I fooling? The natural, authoritative, soothing sound covering up a frail spirit. I'd never had the courage to be subversive, and despite the freedom I knew awaited me I could not subvert my relationship with Sarah.

Or so I thought.

CHAPTER 7

The rest of the Tahoe trip was uneventful. We skied the next two days. I spent most of my time with Donny. We were at about the same level skiing-wise and he had a natural gambling curiosity. Sharon acted as if nothing had happened and I played along. I sensed our encounter would be enough for her, at least for now. I didn't give it much thought. It was something that happened and unless she confronted me I'd try and forget it.

"I'm pregnant."
"What?"
"I'm having an abortion."
"Just like that, huh?"
"You have no say. It's my choice."
"Can we talk about this?"
"It's settled. There's nothing to talk about."
"Be reasonable. I love you, Sarah. I know things haven't been great between us lately but we can work things out.

We could have the baby. If you just give us a chance I know we could make it work."

"I told you I've made my decision."

"Fuck that! Did you hear what I just said? I love you!" How many times had I said those words over the years? I-LOVE-YOU. What did I mean? Maybe I really meant, *I crave you. I despise you making me want you. I'm obsessed with fucking you. Please don't leave me.* I didn't know. It just seemed to be my last play.

"You are blind, aren't you, Martin? Wake up. Things haven't been good with us since the beginning. We've been together about a year. That's plenty of time to know if it's right. And it's not right."

"What about Sonoma?"

"We've had our moments. It was good for awhile, but now it's not. Face it. The bad times far out number the good."

"What are you saying?"

"I'm moving in with Paige for now. I can't stay here any longer."

"What? You jump from one thing to the next, don't you? What is it with you? Why do you constantly have to be hurting people? That girl's in love with you. Moving in with her will just give her false hope."

"Like it gave you false hope? There are no sure bets. You know that. Paige is a friend. She has no expectations. She's helping me out because I need help. I need to get out of here. Don't you understand that? Can't you respect that?"

"Who's being blind, Sarah? I know your game. The tormented princess having to tolerate the injustices of her pitiful life. You're scared. You're running away from me because you don't want to get close to *anyone.* It has to do with your father. He died and left and you and there was no one you were closer with, so now you're scared to love, to *really* love anyone. I understand, Sarah. Please, let's try and work through this."

"Leave my father out of this." She clinched her jaw. "It has nothing to do with him. It's you, Martin. I don't love you. Got it? You're too needy. You're not what you appear to be. You're not honest with yourself about who you are. Shit, you don't even know who you are. I sure as hell don't know you. I just know that I have to get out of this apartment before I go crazy."

"You're already crazy! How can you say those things when all I've ever done is given to you? I've taken care of you. When you come home at three o'clock in the morning all coked out, stinking of bourbon, who's there for you? Who had that shit car of yours fixed? Who's taken you on trips, made fucking great meals, held your hand when you were sick, put your needs ahead of mine? Have you ever once said 'thank you' for anything I've done for you? Have you ever once showed an ounce of gratitude? No. Why? Because you're a selfish, spoiled bitch."

"Yeah? And you're a weak boy. Don't give me that martyr shit! No one does what they don't want to do. You do things for me because you're afraid of losing me. Because you adore me and you're scared. I know, Martin. I can feel it. It's not what I want. I need a man. I need someone strong. Not a weak boy! And you're a weak pathetic little boy, Martin."

The hate that had been stagnating beneath each nerve ending was suddenly liberated. First, it was with a look that struck Sarah like shrapnel. She took it in like sustenance.

Her head tilted back slightly, her square shoulders sloped, and the bold, rigid stance she had assumed throughout our exchange turned pliable. She became passive. Then she said in a whisper, "You want to hit me, don't you?"

I leaned forward and struck her full force with my fist.

Her scream was filled with both terror and ecstasy. Then I hit her again. And again. She fell to the floor, her lip bloody, then staggered back to her feet. She challenged my resolve with a malignant glare. Once again I succumbed to her will. I grabbed the back of her head by her tasseled hair and pulled her lips to mine. I tore open her denim shirt, ripping off the metal buttons. Then I yanked down her jeans, picked her up, and flung her onto the back of my sofa.

I spread her legs and plunged my just released penis into her accommodating sex. A guttural moan belched from deep inside the inferno of her innards escaping through her entire being, out her white skin, her electrically charged silk hair, her green eyes, her scornful mouth. She thrashed about daring me to overpower her. I held her head back by her hair, my arm pushing into the side of her face. I wrapped my other arm around her waist and pulled her toward me while I thrust with all my strength.

We were both lost. Lost in the pain. Lost in the flames of our bliss. Lost in the love, for it was love. A love familiar to us both.

CHAPTER 8

Little Martin never thought of the beatings. He couldn't. He was just a young boy riding with his beautiful dark-skinned mother in their eight-year-old Volkswagen Bug.

"Marty, I have something to tell you."

"Yeah, Ma."

"I'm pregnant. I'm going to have a baby." His mother had always been very open about sex. She told Marty where babies came from when he was five. Initially he thought it sounded strange when she told him the f-word was a bad way of describing sex. She told him about the dogs that used to do it all the time in her neighborhood when she was a girl. Over time he accepted the idea that grown-ups did it, but he never imagined himself ever having sex. His first thought when she broke the news was, *Is it dad's?* His parents had continued spending time together since they had split. This would surely get them back together. But quickly he berated himself for wishful thinking. As if reading his mind, his mother told him everything.

"The father is Bud Cianci. We slept together a few times. I was off the pill for a while. I don't love him. I don't even like him now. He's an asshole. I told him about the baby and he told me to get an abortion. He said he'd deny it was his.

"But I don't care, I want the baby. What do you think, Marty?"

"Why did you go off the pill?"

"It's not healthy to be on it all the time. I took a chance sleeping with him. Do you think I should have an abortion?"

He thought before answering. This would add to their isolation as a family. It was 1968 and the Summer of Love was lingering, but in middle-class suburban Los Angeles, illegitimacy was hidden. Only outcasts got pregnant that weren't married. Martin also sensed the burden that would be placed on *him*. His mother had many lovers during those days, but she blamed men for most of her problems. Marty was too young to be a man in her eyes, but male enough for her to adore. She counted on him and needed him. And he would never fail to be there for her.

"No. I want you to have the baby. We'll be okay."

"It'll be hard. You'll have to help me."

"I know. Don't worry, we'll be fine."

"My sweet boy. My dear, sweet boy."

"I love you too, Mom."

The day had arrived. Laura Fante was coming home from the hospital. She'd spent four days in Valley Lutheran. Martin had stayed with Michael and his family. Michael's stepfather had taken Laura to the hospital after she woke Marty up in the middle of the night. He quickly phoned J. T., who arrived a few minutes later.

They had been four long days for Martin. He hadn't

been allowed to the hospital to visit and only talked to his mother once on the phone. The baby was a girl and both would be coming home Thursday.

Martin couldn't concentrate at school that day. He had friends in class but no one close enough to confide in about the pregnancy. He wanted to tell someone that his baby sister was coming home for the first time. If his mother had been married, it would have been cause for a celebration with his teacher most likely making an announcement to the class. All day he daydreamed. He thought about what she would look like, what it would be like to hold her. He tried to imagine how she would smell. He wondered if she'd be round and pudgy like other babies he'd seen and how much hair she would have. At lunch he ate by himself, then played kickball halfheartedly. Finally the last bell rang and he bolted out of the classroom. He ran the entire eight blocks home.

When he arrived and opened the door he barely noticed his mother lying on the couch in her pajamas. He went straight into her bedroom and looked in the garage-sale-purchased crib. No baby! He ran out to the living room and looked in the bassinet near the front the door. He lifted up the crocheted pink blanket his grandmother had made. Nothing. He looked at his mother and demanded, "Where is she?" Before she had a chance to answer he noticed her blue, beat-up suitcase standing next to the sofa. "Is she in there?"

Laura laughed, "No, she's not here."

"Where is she?"

"She's sick. Nothing serious. They want to keep her in the hospital for a few more days to keep an eye on her, make sure everything's alright."

"Why shouldn't everything be alright? What's wrong?"

"She was was born very small, less than six pounds and

she's having a little trouble breathing. She'll be fine in a day or two. Don't worry." She reached for a cigarette on the coffee table. "Marty, get me some matches please. I think there's some in the kitchen."

"You don't need a cigarette. When are you going to quit?"

"Don't start that. I'm weak right now. I can barely move. Just do what your mother says."

"Do you want to die of cancer?"

"Come on, kid. Just get me the matches, please."

The baby arrived three days later, on a Sunday. Martin had never seen such a tiny human being. She was darker than he was, with black eyes. And she was hairy. Black fuzz covered her little body and the hair on her head, a good three inches long, stuck straight up. It was soft and Martin liked to touch it. At first he was apprehensive about holding her but his mother showed him how to cradle the baby in his arms. "Hold her under this arm, and let her head rest on your other arm. Here, hold her head in your hand. That's it. Look, she's smiling at you."

Their lives became the child. Laura did not nurse so Martin bottle-fed her formula whenever he was at home. He changed her and rocked her and sang to her when she cried. There was a neighbor boy who used to come around, a twelve-year-old tough who Martin's mother had a soft spot for. When he saw the baby for the first time he said, "It looks like a monkey."

Martin jumped him. "Don't call her a monkey. She's not a monkey, you idiot!"

The scraggly-haired adolescent laughed and fended off Martin's punches with little effort. "Sorry, but it looks like a little monkey. Doesn't it?"

"She's not an 'it.' Her name is Anna and she's not a monkey, you dickhead!"

After a few months she had lost the fuzz and her hair was long enough that most people assumed she was a girl. Her eyes got clearer and her skin was smooth and soft. Martin thought she was the most beautiful thing he had ever seen.

"Holy shit!"
"What is it? What's happening, Mom?"
"It's an earthquake."
"Are we going to die?"
"I don't know, son. Come on, we need to get under the doorway. Grab your sister."

The earth rolled and gyrated under the bed. Marty had slept with Laura that night. He bounced out of bed and picked up his sister from the crib. She might have slept on through the earth shaking if Marty hadn't grabbed her and started running for the door, stumbling and tipping like a drunk. The windows rattled.

The cupboards slammed open and closed with the dishes and glasses and Tupperware flying through the kitchen slamming against the wall, or sink, or tile floor. Was this it? Was this death, so soon? Martin hoped not. As they opened the front door they were drenched. The apartment building swimming pool, not ten feet from their front door, had turned into a mini-tsunami. They stood there huddled together, as wet as if they'd been in a downpour.

Thirty-two seconds after it started the earthquake was over. It wasn't the big one, although it had been plenty big for Marty. His first "moderate" earthquake measured 6.2 on the Richter scale. There was a eerie quite moment after the temblor ceased. The still of dawn but with no whispers or rustling from nature or man. No early morning sparrows chirping, no cars humming by, no humans chattering. Martin felt a strange calm and peace. It was if the world had stopped and he had walked onto a cloud. He wasn't afraid.

In fact he felt strong and very much alive. His senses were sharp. He felt the urge to call his best friend. And then the tornado of human activity descended.

The sirens first and then the neighbors. Like gophers coming out of their holes, all the building's tenants scampered out of their apartments. Toni Casas and her three kids lived in 210. They were the first to arrive at Martin's apartment. "Is anyone hurt? How's the baby?"

"We're okay," replied Laura.

"Can you believe it? Our TV was thrown halfway across the room like a football. I heard on the news that the Sepulveda dam might be damaged and that they may have to evacuate. So you better pack up some things."

Dazed, Laura Fante hadn't heard a word. "What?"

"The Sepulveda dam. It's cracked. The water from all the rain in the reservoir may spill onto the streets. The police say be prepared to leave. Do you have anywhere to go?"

"I don't know. My mother's, I suppose."

"You better call her then. The phone lines are getting all tied up. You'll be lucky to get through."

They spent two weeks at Laura's mother's house.

One morning Martin's grandmother offered to take the baby for the day. She had never learned to drive. She took the stroller and left on foot. She planned on going to the bank and the grocery store then to visit a friend from church. Before she left, Martin heard the two women arguing in Spanish. He understood little but picked up that his grandmother was not happy with the way Laura was raising her children. He would try to stay clear of his mother while his grandmother was gone.

Martin ate breakfast then left to explore the alley behind the house. When he was gone, his mother cleaned up the dishes then sat on the rocking chair in the living room. She turned on the TV and watched a succession of game shows. Then she decided to clean the house. With the television still on she got up and vacuumed, cleaned the bathroom, scrubbing bathtub, sink and toilet. After that she mopped the kitchen floor and did a load of laundry. She began muttering to herself. "My fucking mother. She has no idea how hard it is. All she does is criticize and judge me. I hate her. I hate the bitch. I wish the shriveled up old witch would die. How dare she judge me. How dare she tell me how to raise my kids. Bitch! What did my father ever see in that wretched woman?"

"Mom?"

"It's about time that little brat came back. Where the fuck has he been? Fucking brat just takes off."

"Where are you?" Marty came in through the back door into the kitchen, made his way into the living room, and headed toward the back bedrooms. He had discovered an apricot tree and brought back a load tied in his shirt. "Oh, here you are."

He sensed her rage and without thinking attempted to disarm her. "I found an apricot tree and didn't have a bag so I made one out of my shirt. Have an apricot. They taste great."

"What are you, stupid? The shirt is ruined." She grabbed the bundle out of his hands. "Do you know how much money it takes to buy your clothes? To keep your little ass covered? Well let me tell you, brat. It takes dollars. Dollars I don't have. Dollars I work hard for, so you can ruin everything. You little monster!" And she hit him on the side of the head with the apricot-filled shirt. He fell straight down to his knees and covered up. She hit him again crushing a number of the apricots. Some of the mangled fruit spilled from the makeshift bag and smashed into Martin's face. He could taste the sweetness as the air filled with the fragrance of the ripe apricots. She pummeled him.

"Please, Mom, don't hit me," he cried out, at which point she threw the mass of smashed fruit at his head. Then she grabbed him by his belt and pulled him toward her, slapping him in the face as she screamed. "Little bastard! You don't appreciate anything, do you? I don't get any fucking help. Your goddamned father walked out on us. Your fucking grandmother is a cunt!" Then she hurled the boy down onto the floor and continued slapping with both hands before turning and racing out of the house yelling, "I get no help. I get no fucking help from anyone. No one gives a shit. FUCK ALL OF YOU!"

CHAPTER 9

The sunlight streaming through the bedroom window woke us both up. Sarah had held on to me for most of the night. It seemed natural and routine although it had been months since she had displayed such affection. I felt her breath on my neck, and opened my eyes to see her looking at me. "Te quiero," she whispered. Who was I to question her love? To try to understand how a violent encounter the previous night had metamorphosed into this painful tenderness? We were both waking into consciousness out of a contented, fulfilling sleep. Embracing in my bed we said nothing. Our feelings flowed into a sea of understanding. We had known each other for centuries. There was no telling where her flesh ended and mine began. Her leg was my leg. Her arm wrapped around my neck with her hand draped onto my chest was part of the single sculpture of our body. My mind was empty. My touch was complete. We had crashed and now we were basking. Like everything before and everything to come, it was transient. That was the trick though: to be in the feeling with the awareness that it would vanish as certainly as it had appeared. An acceptance of what was soon to be just another memory.

The phantom of love was as real as the eucalyptus trees in the Presidio or the homeless men curled up in the hideaway spaces on the city streets. But like the wind, it was attainable only in relation to what was still, and we were as still as the sun's rays. Sarah's beauty laid in her delicate and refined complexity. The ambivalence of her consciousness embraced the pain and frivolity of my spirit.

We stayed in bed until the sun's direct light had made its way past my window. I suggested we walk to Grant Street and have coffee at the North Beach Cafe. She agreed. We walked mostly in silence. As awareness of our past together and our present situation began infiltrating my thoughts, the feelings of panic and frustration made their insidious reentry. I kept a cool veneer but Sarah was too close not to sense the ripple in our momentary bliss. Over coffee we discussed our options without venom. I clicked into the objective reporter mode. I knew our time together was coming to an end. As we talked I suppressed all the emotions behind that fact. Something deep inside told me I was fighting for my life. Of course my rationale would not allow any of that to surface.

The thought of me begging Sarah to stay flashed in the neon of my mind but disappeared immediately. If I was fighting for my life then begging would surely be the dagger that would kill me. As always death seemed a breath away.

"We can't stay together, you know that?"

"I know."

"We'll die if we stay together."

"What about the baby?"

"I'm late, but I'm not sure that I'm pregnant."

I didn't need to ask why she had lied. I already knew. In

that moment I realized just how much alike we were. We were both groping for something in the other that couldn't be given. She had reached for that place in me that was buried under all the violence: the violence of my child-hood, the violence of my love, the violence of my repressed violence. She had gotten a taste of the wonderful abandon that lay beneath the ignored torment. The only way she could spark it was through the violence, the beautiful, con-suming violence.

The place in her that knew about me knew not from logic but from feeling, by understanding and recognition. For fear of seeing the source of that recognition I dared not ask how she understood so clearly the core of the violence. How could she relate so intimately unless our experiences were fused in some way, unless she had lived what I had lived? We had never spoken of our childhoods. It now seemed clear why. I felt the sudden urge to run.

How could I run from the source of my ecstasy? Run from the mystery that kept my life vibrant and exciting? Not moments earlier I had fantasized about begging her to stay. Now I wanted her gone. But I'm an adult and I can't run, so I sprinted from awareness, from the consciousness that threatened me like a warrant for my arrest. I started writing a radio news story in my mind. *Be concise and factu-al. The key is accuracy and objectivity. No longer than thirty seconds.* I conversed with Sarah about her moving in with Paige and the other details associated with breaking-up while I typed "our story" on the computer keyboard in my head.

I started with a catchy lead:

"She gave me for my pains a world of sighs." Shakespeare couldn't have said it better when describing the relationship of a San Francisco couple who today decided to call it quits. Thirty-

three-year-old Martin Fante and thirty-one-year-old Sarah Demkowski parted friends after both decided that their personal demons best be left alone—buried to fester. When interviewed by UNS News both refused comment about the other. But sources close to the couple say the two often argued violently. The relationship lasted thirteen months. Demkowski says she plans on moving out of Fante's Russian Hill apartment and will live with a friend until she gets back on her feet.

We sat there drinking our coffee and tuning out in unison. I had no fight left in me. No panic or sense of loss, just garbled reception from my psyche: a gray cloud of dulled emotion. We agreed to a clean break to give our battered feelings time to sort things out. But as she said those words, "sort things out," I came to the realization that "things" would never be sorted out. My life would always be unresolved no matter how hard I tried to bring closure.

CHAPTER 10

"You've got such a cute little butt, Marty."

"Mom!"

"Well, you do. Do you have any hair on it?"

"Come on, Laura."

"Just a few hairs? Maybe it's getting bushy like it does on Mexican men. Do you have any pubic hair yet?"

"No, Mother."

"None? I bet you've got a few. Your voice is starting to change."

"Nope, not a one. You happy?"

"Really? Let's see. Come on, drop 'em."

"If you don't stop, I'm leaving."

"You know you couldn't, even if you tried."

"Why's that?"

"You know what's simmering on the stove right now?"

"Chicken mole?"

"You got it, kid. Now come over here and give your mother a kiss."

"Food for the Gods to tempt the Devil himself. You are a vixen, mother."

"Vixen? Where did you learn such a word? You're too smart for your own good."

Laura had just completed her first semester of college. She had gone back to school to study psychology and had made the Dean's list with a 3.75 GPA. She was ready to celebrate and she couldn't think of anyone she wanted to be with more than her ten-year-old son. Martin was convinced she was the best cook on the planet. Both his grandmothers were excellent cooks. His Italian grandmother made a mean eggplant parmigiana; her pastries were mouth-watering masterpieces. And his Mexican grandmother had the gift of making simple pinto beans grand and satisfying. But his mother took both traditions and like an artist she improvised to make extraordinary, lustful meals. And she did it mostly with simple ingredients. Martin had learned early on that in this respect he was blessed. He would rather have his mother's tortillas and eggs than any fancy sit down dinner he might eat at a friend's.

And it wasn't just family bias. Young Martin had developed a discriminating palate. His friends also preferred his mother's cooking. Whenever they had the chance, which was often since Laura loved cooking for people who liked her food, they would come to Martin's for dinner. And when his friends' mothers asked for her recipes, his buddies still preferred Laura's cooking. Like any true master her work could be copied but never duplicated. Martin appreciated all her cooking but the two meals that put him at her mercy were rigatoni and chicken mole. He could count on rigatoni every year on his birthday. The chicken mole was always a surprise.

As the two of them sat eating Martin noticed that his sister wasn't around. "Where's Anna?"

"She's at Candi's. Candi is taking her for the night."

"*Really?*"

"Remember last week we had Kimberly? Well, this week your sister is staying with them. We've worked out an agreement to give each other a break every now and then." Candi was Martin's mother's new friend from school. The two had met in class and discovered they had a lot in common.

Both were single parents. Both were feminists. Together they had joined the L.A. chapter of NOW. The slightly overweight Candi had short blond hair with bangs cut just above her eyes. Martin thought she had a radiant smile. She was one of few adults that treated him with respect. She related to him as an intelligent individual despite his small stature and youth. He liked her. She was a lesbian. She had recently come out, divorcing her husband and moving to California from Wisconsin. She had a butch lover named Pam.

"Listen, Marty, I know you're going through this prepubescent thing where you don't want to hang out with your mother, and I respect that, but we haven't spent much time together lately and I wanted to celebrate getting through my first semester. I thought maybe we could go to a movie tonight?"

"Sure, Ma, what do you have in mind?"

"There's this movie playing at the LaReina called *King of Hearts*. I think you'll like it."

The LaReina was one of few special places reserved for just Martin and his mother.

Marty never suggested that theater when he went to the movies with his friends. It was unspoken that the two would go there only with each other, not with his sister, not even with special men like his father. The LaReina was the only movie house of its kind in the valley. It showed offbeat and foreign films. She had taken him there to see Bergman's *The Seventh Seal* as well as *Easy Rider* and *La Strada*. "What's it about?"

"It's a French movie that takes place during World War I."

"It's a war movie?" That seemed strange. His mother had developed an elaborate strategy to prove that Martin was a pacifist. If he was ever drafted he could claim rightfully to be a conscientious objector. She made him promise not to fight, a promise he broke nearly every week at school. She never bought him guns or war toys, yet he was fascinated with World War II weaponry and aircraft. He was always assembling models of fighting planes from all sides: Japanese Zeros, German Stutkas, American Flying Tigers, British Spitfires. She didn't clamp down too hard on the boy, but she pressured him by telling him that she prayed he wouldn't go to war.

"Strong young men sent off, returning home dead or different. Your uncle Reuben was changed by Vietnam. He's become bitter and hostile. Remember how he was before the war? War changes people and not for the better. It makes people mean. That won't happen to you, Marty."

"I thought you didn't want me to see war movies?"

"This one's different. You'll like it."

Martin had no doubt.

Filebroc
et
Les Productions
Artistes Associees
presentent
Pierre Brasseur
Genevieve Bujold
et
Alan Bates
LE ROI DES COEURS
(king of hearts)

The young boy sat in the darkened movie theater chomping on his extra buttered popcorn and getting lost in the movie. The film grabbed hold of his imagination like no other movie he'd ever seen. The French setting, the sub-titles, the eccentricities of the characters all worked their romantic magic, taking him to an enchanted, strangely beautiful world. He longed to be on the front lines with the kilt-clad Scottish soldiers. He wished he was playing cards with the residents of the lunatic asylum. He wanted to possess the spiked helmet of the German general.

It was through the setting and the people that the antiwar theme made its lasting impression. In later years Martin would go to revival houses and see the film at every opportunity.

The absurdity of war, a land where the insane are more compassionate and full of life than the so-called normal people, love being the precursor to all that was admirable and hopeful: all simple themes done before a million times. But in *King of Hearts* they were handled with a beautiful simplicity that seemed to speak truth without sentimentality. Martin knew nothing of that. All he knew was that he loved it.

After the movie his mother took him to Foster's Freeze where they ordered separate hot fudge sundaes, his with nuts, hers with an extra cherry. "Did you like the movie?"

"Yeah."

"Why?"

"It was funny. I liked the town's people."

"Do you know why he went back to the insane asylum, naked?"

"Because he didn't want to live in a world with war."

"That's right, And because he had never experienced such deep love and understanding of what is truly important."

"Like stopping and taking time to enjoy life.

Appreciating things that we take for granted, enjoying and living in the moment."

"Like when his girlfriend from the asylum told him that three minutes of life was wonderful?"

"Exactly. She opened his heart. This crazy, tiny woman who wore a ridiculous tutu opened his heart and educated him to love."

They drove home. They took turns using the bathroom to clean up before going to bed. It was late. "Do you want to sleep with me tonight, Marty?"

"Don't you think I'm a little old for that?"

"No one has to know."

"Okay."

CHAPTER 11

I've always maintained that good cursing can be like poetry. As a kid growing up I was envious of the way certain people could weave the perfect curse words with just the right cadence and emphasis into a story or situation that called for strength. My father was a master. *Motherfucker* and *cocksucker* were his favorites. The real talent comes in using those words with just the right combination of authority, vulgarity, and irony. My father is a big man and can intimidate people with his size despite the fact that he can charm most people with an easy going Brooklynesque, fun-loving personality. But don't piss him off. His special cursing talent enables him to tell someone to fuck themselves and have that person walking away thanking him. When I was sixteen, an Iranian mechanic who had worked on his car told him that he could fix my beat-up old Honda Civic for under $200. When I went to pick up the car the bill came to $315. "What's this?" I asked. He started explaining that he had to resurface the flywheel and do this and that and a bunch of other things that went over my head.

My father had come down to meet me. I told him the situation. He tried to reason with the fellow. "You said you could fix it for two hundred dollars. How about we pay you the two hundred and call it even?"

The guy couldn't be reasoned with. "Listen Al, I tried—"

"No, you listen, motherfucker! You said two hundred dollars; that's what we're paying you. And if the car doesn't run like Jim Thorpe, if it breaks down within the next six months, I'm coming back here and sticking that tire iron up your ass. Okay? Pay the man, kid." The mechanic was a big guy, but he was petrified. He started laughing sheepishly. He ended up throwing in an oil change and a tune-up for the original $200. Afterward my father questioned out loud: "Why do people force you to treat them that way?"

I admired the way my father could wield that power on command. Whenever I got in a similar situation, when I cursed, my adversary would usually laugh, but not sheepishly. As a youngster I almost always would end up fighting, not wanting to back down no matter how imposing the guy was. And I usually lost.

Later I learned to talk my way out of a fight without losing face, mostly by exhausting my opponent with a cavalcade of logic, so much that he forgot how pissed he was. And besides I never tapped into my killer instinct, until recently.

The other night I came close to cursing perfection. I was in the Mauna Loa, a bar in the Cow Hollow district. I was in the neighborhood and felt like a quick game of pool so I ducked in. I got there about midnight and put my name on the chalkboard. The place was packed, mostly with posers and yuppie drug dealers. I got lucky and won a string of games. Most of the competition was drunk. This one dude I beat three times kept bad-mouthing me while I played: *"That's a real tough shot. I'm going to the bathroom, don't touch my beer! You ain't that good, just lucky."* The guy was an idiot. He played pool like a blind man; he had no eye and all his movements were herky-jerky.

I didn't pay him that much mind until on his fourth try he started laughing and saying he was going to kick my ass. "Keep talking, pal," I said.

"I'll kick your ass, man. You want to put a wager on it?"

"Whatever you say."

I reached into my pocket and pulled out two twenties. I put them on the table. "Okay, pal, get it up."

He sneered, looked down at the money, hesitated, then picked up the forty dollars and put it in his pocket. He walked over to a bar stool in the corner across from the table and sat down. I walked over to him and asked, "What are you doing, moron?"

"I changed my mind. I don't feel like playing."

"Give me my money back, dogmeat."

"Your loss, *pal!*"

I saw red. I got into his face and let it roll, "Listen, motherfucker, if you don't take the money out of your pants and hand it over right now, I'll have to take this cue stick and wrap it around your fat, ugly head!"

He stood up, "What was that?"

The punk was a good four inches taller than I am and outweighed me by at least fifty pounds. "You heard me, *cocksucker!*"

No response, just a dumb look. A friend of his, another punk who also was a lot bigger than me, came over and asked, "What did you say?"

Now I had the twin towers, a pair of cretins hovering over me like two stupid lost kids. "This is not your business, Jack. If I were you, I'd turn around and sit back down."

He looked up, then pointed to a sign above the pool table that read: NO WAGERING. "Hey, there's no gambling in here!"

"You're gambling with your health, motherfucker." He looked up at his buddy, who gave him a look that said, *I can handle this*. Then he turned and headed toward the bar. The other asshole just stood there looking at me with his mouth half open. I looked at him squarely in his big empty, gray eyes and demanded my money. "Now, dickhead!" He went back to his stool and sat down like nothing was happening. I grabbed a pool stick. I figured I had to equalize the situation. Just as I started my backswing his friend jumped me from behind, knocking the pool cue out of my hands.

I quickly escaped his grip and jumped the other fool, who was, oddly enough, still sitting. I hit him with three quick rights to his flat, dumbstruck face before he staggered up and swung a big, lumbering roundhouse right. I easily avoided his punches and began pounding on his midsection. The bar's customers scurried like hookers spotting a squad car. Next thing I knew I was being grabbed by two big oafs: the doorman and the bartender. "Cool down, man!" I heard one of them say. So finally I stopped. My opponent stood not two feet from me, lip bloodied and weary. But he mustered a contemptuous stare and with the bartender gripping me from behind, he threw a weak right that connected down the side of my face, from temple to chin. Round two.

I slipped the burly bartender's brutish bear hug and went for the punk's legs. I lifted all 200-plus pounds and slammed him down on the bar. I reached for a glass to smash into his face, but came up empty. I began slugging his gut and reaching up attempting to get in a few head punches. I rammed my hand into his pocket and grabbed some money. I don't think he realized what I did because he was just laid there, stunned. Then I was in a pile of bodies.

The bartender, the doorman, and two enthusiastic customers had pulled me off the brute.

It's a bit fuzzy after that, but I remember trying to reason with the doorman, asking where the *idiot* was and telling him that the guy had stolen my money. "It's over, man. Calm down!"

"Where is he!" I demanded.

"He's gone! The police are on their way, you better go too. You cool?"

I left the bar as the police were pulling up. As I walked out I felt as if I was in a Martin Scorsese movie: slow motion as I glanced at the frozen customers staring at me in disbelief. Their expressions ran an array from admiration and fear to disgust. One guy patted me on the back as I headed out the door. "Way to go, bud!" I heard a fat woman in too-tight jeans mutter, "Animal." As I walked into the night I felt an electric buzz. I felt like celebrating with friends. I felt like making love.

As quickly as the euphoria had set in it turned to melancholia. I thought of Sarah.

If she had been with me she no doubt would have jumped in. We could have laughed about it then made love. I missed her.

I was too amped to go home so I wandered the streets.

I walked up Polk to the Polk Street Tavern, a smoky dive, and had two bourbon and waters in honor of Sarah. Soon after I was back on the frenetic city streets. I wandered up Polk Street. I stopped in a 24-hour tobacco shop near Broadway and bought a pack of Hav-a-Tampas, I lit one and continued walking.

At Pine Street the boy prostitutes were soliciting, strung out and tricking for their next fix. I saw one boy— he couldn't have been more than fourteen—get in the backseat of a white Mercedes. His eyes were blank and his long blond hair was stringy: a street cherub being consumed by some rich baby bugger, probably an upstanding, well respected citizen. A cop friend of mine once told me that they had one night caught a local sportscaster attempting to buy such a boy. The rich prick pleaded with the cops to let him go. It would ruin his career and reputation. They gave him a warning. They were sports fans.

I was still pumped, and horny. I thought about calling Sarah but decided against it. I stopped in another bar and had two more bourbons instead. I was drunk. I left the bar and as I started walking I got a hard-on. I meandered my way toward North Beach thinking that the walk and cool air would suppress my libido. I was wrong. The more I walked, the hornier I got. I decided a visit to the Lusty Lady was in order. I walked in to a booth with three dollars worth of quarters and started feeding the machine. The black, wooden partition made its way up over my window to reveal three naked girls dancing. One saw my booth open for business and made her way to my window.

She was tall with short black hair and wore red high heel pumps. She had thick lips and bad skin. Her pussy was smooth, white, and shaven. She moved well to the pump-action, acid jazz dance music that blared from inside the echo chamber of the mirrored strip cage. When she got to my window she looked into my eyes and gave me a *fuck me* smile.

I grinned back at which time she swiveled her narrow hips not an inch from the window. She took her hands and parted her hairless cunt. She moved in close enough so that her light brown labia barely kissed the glass. She was staring at me when she began gyrating. Then she quickly looked away. She was about six inches from my nose but might as well have been a hologram. But I didn't care, I was getting my three dollars worth: *You unlock this door with the key of imagination. Your next stop. . . the vaginal zone.* I smiled then imagined putting my tongue up her vagina then flicking it gently across her clitoris. She turned around and bent over and again parted her vaginal lips, barely fingering the outside of her hole. The partition started coming down as my penis went back up. I frantically re-fed the machine with the last of my quarters. Then my time was up.

It was nearly 2A.M., just enough time to hit one last bar. I cruised over to Specs on Columbus and downed two more bourbon and waters. When the bar closed, I was off my ass. I stumbled out but to my chagrin I was still horny.

Fuck it, I thought. I'm not going home and jerking off. I looked up and saw the sign. In big yellow neon:

DRAGOON: ORIENTAL MASSAGE.

I hit the buzzer outside the caged entry, "Yes?" came back the Asian-sounding female voice.

"Are you still open?"

"You have money?"

"Not much, about twenty dollars."

"We close."

"I have American Express."

"We take 'Mer'can 'Spress. Okay, you come down now." I opened the metal door and descended a flight of stairs, where there was a closed purple door. It opened immediately and there stood a Vietnamese woman about 5'2", a bit chunky with a too-short, too-tight black Lycra skirt. She smiled big and said, "Hello. Come this way." I followed her down a long narrow hallway. Both walls had cheap, off-white wallpaper; the carpet was thick and red. She led me into a room halfway down the hall.

I looked up and saw velvet pictures of naked ladies lining the walls. To my right there was a long, brown leather sofa. On it were six Vietnamese women sitting and smiling at me. The woman who had escorted me asked me my name. I told her. "Welcome, Martin. These ah the girls. This is Vicki, this is Becky, this is Patty, this is Paula, this is Jackie, and this is Teddy. Which one you like?"

I was too drunk to make an informed, rational decision so I chose the only name I remembered. "I'll take Vicki."

"Good! Vicki very nice."

Vicki immediately stood up, took my hand, and walked me out the room down the hallway. Where I thought the hallway ended there was another corridor. We turned right and walked down the darkened hallway. I was getting a lot of exercise. Finally we reached a door. Vicki took out a key and unlocked it. The room was in complete darkness. She pulled me in by the hand and turned on a lamp then dimmed the light.

As I walked in I felt an odd comfort. The outside world seemed far away. The room was warm. Below dark wallpaper a single mattress lay on the floor in the corner. A Shower Massage head attached to a silver coil was laying on the bathtub fixtures. I suddenly felt tired, relaxed. Vicki flashed a childlike smile and told me to get undressed and lie under the sheets. I was charmed by her simple and tender directions. Somehow she sensed that I had never done this before. In this hard world there are angels everywhere; knowing how to be open to them without guilt or regret is the trick to survival. She left the room and came back a few minutes later in a navy blue silk robe. I was lying on my back when she reentered the room. How pure and clean she looked. She lit three candles on a small table near the bathtub and came over to me. "Turn over, Martin. I give you massage now." I turned on my stomach and closed my eyes. She rubbed her hands together, warming some oil then began to stroke my neck. It was not a deep massage. In fact it wasn't a massage in the strictest sense. Her movements were light and slow. She rubbed me from head to feet, then told me to turn over. Then she rubbed my front in much the same fashion, not giving my cock any special treatment but not ignoring it.

I wasn't horny anymore. Wouldn't you know it? It remained limp but her hands felt nice anyway. I breathed in, smelling lavender from her massage oil. I was drunk but relaxed. My head was spinning only slightly. I liked the sensation: it added to the celestial feel. She stopped after rubbing my toes and came up close to my face. "What mo' you want, Martin?"

"What more you got, Vicki?"

"Anything you want?"

"How about the big one?"

"Yes, I do the big one for you."

She took off her robe and got under the sheets with me. I lay there content as a dog on the beach as she started playing with my cock. It remained limp. "I drank a lot tonight, Vicki."

"That's okay, Martin, don't worry." Then she put my limp penis in her mouth. She was very good and soon I was hard. She slipped on a condom then sat on top of me. She was wet, which surprised me. I thought it was just a job to them. Perhaps it was a trick, but I felt like she was enjoying it.

She rocked gently as I reached up and cupped her breasts. They seemed rigid and a bit large for her frame, but I didn't mind. I moaned and closed my eyes.

I was too drunk to come. After what seemed a very long, enjoyable time of her on top, I decided I wanted to. Without pulling out, I sat up, put my arms around Vicki, and upturned her on her back. I started pumping as I kissed her neck and grabbed her ass. Then I closed my eyes and allowed myself to orgasm.

I rolled off and lay next to her for a while. After a few

minutes of silence she said, "Come on, Martin, let's take a bath."

"No thanks, I don't want a bath."

"I promise, you like bath."

"Okay."

She walked me to the tub, turned on the water, checked the temperature, then told me to sit down. She proceeded to give me the best bath I'd ever had. As she soaped me up and rinsed me off she began talking in a soft voice. "You a good lover, Martin."

I looked up at her and almost started crying. "Thank you, Vicki. What's your real name?"

"Lee Quan."

"You're from Vietnam. How long have you been here, Lee Quan?"

"Ten years. I'm from Hanoi. I came here to be with family."

"Do you like it here?" It was a horrible question and I regretted asking it immediately. She gave me an intense look, and let down her subtle and gentle guard, enabling me to get an ephemeral glimpse of the real Lee Quan, the sad and dispossessed Lee Quan. With a hint of youthful hope she said, "I like San Francisco."

"So do I," I said, wanting to embrace her and take her home, rescue her from an existence that was unworthy of her. Marry her. Take care of her. Love her. Desire bled into an urge to connect. Human longing—I hated it. I'd worked to obliterate it. To pummel it into submission. But it always came back, and under the strangest circumstances.

I suppose ultimately I preferred desolation to numbness.

When I got to my apartment I went straight to the bedroom and turned on the wall lamp. I looked down and saw a body under my white comforter. It was Sarah. She looked up. "Hi."

"How'd you get in?"

"The fire escape. Your window was open."

I crawled in bed, dead tired and wanting nothing but the peace of sleep. But Sarah's warmth brought my body back to life. She gently touched my face, then kissed my cheek. I put my head on her breast and listened. The beating of her heart let me know everything was all right.

In the morning she was gone.

CHAPTER 12

It was 11:30 on a Sunday night when the phone rang. It was Sharon. "Hi, Marty, I'm sorry for calling so late, I didn't realize how late it was until I just noticed as I was dialing. We can talk tomorrow."

"No, that's okay. I was just sitting here watching *Eyes On the Prize* for the twentieth time."

"What's *Eyes On the Prize?* "

"It's a series on the civil rights movement."

"Sounds interesting."

"Yeah, they were just getting to the assassination of Martin Luther King."

"You sure I'm not disturbing you?"

"No. Like I said, I've seen it several times. I taped it. Besides this part always depresses me."

"I remember when it happened."

"Really?"

"Yeah. I was living in dorms at Berkeley. I was alone studying in my room when I heard a scream. I went out in the hall and people started coming out of their rooms. We went down stairs and there was a group watching the TV. I asked a girl what was going on, and she told me. I was shocked. We all just stood and watched the television in disbelief."

"I was eight at the time."

"Anyway, it's been so crazy at work, I haven't had a chance to talk to you."

"What's up?"

"Your six months are up. We really like the work you're doing and we hoped you'd stay on for at least the additional option period. We've got some ideas for the future and I wanted to bounce them off you."

"Sure."

"I thought we could talk more over dinner one night this week."

My instincts told me agreeing to dinner could lead down the slippery slope of an emotional quagmire, but my palate thought better. "I never turn down a free meal."

We met at Sol Y Luna on Van Ness. We shared a rich, tomatoe paella and a bottle of Spanish wine. We talked mostly about work.

"We really appreciate the job you're doing, Marty. Both Tom and I are very happy that we hired you. Unlike some other employees, one we won't mention, you never seem to get rattled."

"Thank you, Sharon."

"We're hoping that the longer you stay with us, the more our audience will get to know the quality of your work and over time come to trust you even more than they do now. That's very important to us. Our bread and butter is our audience, and we've found over the years they're very loyal. What we'd like to do is sign you to a long-term deal, maybe three years, but we respect you not wanting to do that right now. But your six months are up and we wanted to kick in the option.

"We can't pay you any more money at this point, although we'd like to. But we *are* getting a better medical plan, one that includes dental and eye care. When the year is up we'd like to renegotiate and hopefully raise your salary then." There was an awkward moment of silence. I was hoping maybe she'd throw in a few more compliments. "What do you think?" she said.

I had guessed the content of the meeting and had thought about it beforehand. They put up with my personal phone calls and strolls on the waterfront, as well as my moodiness. They appreciated my work and thought I was a good fit for Family Broadcasting with my relaxed on-air style. These things went a long way for me and despite my early apprehension about working for the Christians I was beginning to feel a sense of ease and belonging with these people. "I'm flattered. I'd be happy to continue working for you."

She looked relieved as she continued the conversation with a directness that opened me yet more to her. "That's great, Marty. You know we really would like to pay you big bucks and hopefully when we get more commercial stations we can."

"If it happens, fine. But I'm not worried. I've had some pretty bad experiences working for the big bucks. It's not like I have anything to show for it except some heartache."

"Heartache?"

"At a country station I once worked at, I was fired right after my morning shift one day. The reason they gave me was that I was 'talking too much.' I was taking time away from the DJ. It was bullshit. About a week a before, the program director had taken me to lunch and told me they had long-term plans for me. After I was fired I heard he had planned to fire me as soon as he took over but waited until the ratings period was over. He lulled me into believing they were going to start contract talks with me. I was working without a contract and it was a non union shop. My next job I brought in the union. I was fired there too, for that."

"You know there's no deception going on here?"

"I know. I never trusted that guy anyway. Some hot-shot hired out of Sacramento to take the station to the 'next level.' He was fired after two books."

"Why did you leave L.A.?"

After a number of smaller market jobs I'd been hired at a Top 40 station down south a few years back. I'm sure that jumped out at Sharon when she read my resume; I was at a top-rated station in the country's number two market. She felt comfortable enough to ask. I felt safe enough to answer honestly.

"I was dating the morning DJ. Jennifer Ryan. We planned on getting married. I practically lived in her Santa Monica loft. She was good on the air, funny, smart, and creative. Her show was the talk of the town for a while appearing on lots of TV and billboards. I was her newsman. We kept our romance secret, she wanted it that way, but people suspected. We never talked about it directly on the air, but we flirted like crazy and it was the buzz among listeners for a while driving up ratings through the roof. We had a four share. But when the ratings dipped she got weird and broke it off and I was fired. Some friends at the station told me later she was behind it. I felt like an idiot. She liked the sex enough, but her career meant everything to her. When the ratings dropped she felt threatened. . . I was young. It was a rude awakening. After that I had to get out of L.A."

"Do you ever talk to her?"

"No. Our break-up wasn't very nice."

"What happened?"

"You don't really want to know this, do you?"

"Yes, I do. I'm interested. Please tell me, Marty."

"She liked pain. She'd ask me to hit and choke her, and other things. Sometimes when I didn't feel like it, later that night or the next day, she'd provoke me. Like come on to some guy at a party or act like bitch. About three weeks after we broke up she called and asked me to go to a play—*Cat On a Hot Tin Roof*. We got drunk before the show and she started grabbing me as we sat and watched that sweaty, smoldering poetry of Tennessee Williams. Afterward, we walked back to her loft, the whole time she was kissing and feeling me. I couldn't wait to get to her place. And then she turned cold. She'd done a good job this time. She knew I was crazy about her and played it beautifully. So I gave her what I thought she wanted all along."

"What was that?"

"What do you think?"

"Tell me."

"I beat her up then we had sex." Suddenly, Sarah was in my head. That was five years ago. I hadn't changed. I was stuck. I had loved Jennifer. It took me two years to get over her. I still wasn't completely free of her. But I hadn't learned a fucking thing! I needed a drink. "Listen, enough about my screwed-up personal life, what do you say we head across the street to U.S.101 for a drink?"

The bar is a dive and the pool tables are crooked. None of the sticks have full tips and most of them are warped. But the juke box has great music and the bartenders are friendly Scottish women. Most of the regulars are drunks. I go there occasionally, but not enough to be a regular.

Sharon liked the bar. She has the admirable quality of feeling at ease wherever she is. I've met few women like that.

She ordered our drinks, a Stoli on the rocks for me and

a beer for her, while I put a dollar in the jukebox and picked four songs: the Beatles' "Dear Prudence," Bob Marley's "Buffalo Soldier," John Lennon's "Jealous Guy," and the Cowboy Junkies' "Walking After Midnight." It was a good mix.

We talked and shot about a dozen games of pool. I was surprised when Sharon said she hadn't played much. She asked me for a few pointers and I obliged. She takes instruction well and can admit to not being good at certain things, qualities in a woman that excite me. She's also a fast learner and ended up beating me two out of the last three games. I enjoyed her company. I'd kept the possibility of bedding her again in the back of mind. She hinted often that she would be available. But as we played pool I decided I wouldn't sleep with her again.

We left the bar and I walked her to her car. We hugged and I kissed her on the cheek. She told me that if there was ever "anything" I needed that she would be there for me. She's a good woman.

An image of me mounting her on her car flashed through my mind; her blue dress up around her waist, my hands up under it on her breasts while we bounced atop her hood. *Take them all. You're a free man, don't dare turn down a fuck, any fuck!* It was screaming at me, only I wasn't sure what It was: Nature? God? Satan? Desperation? Fear? Wonder? Homicide?

I thanked Sharon for dinner and as I walked away I put my hand in my pocket to hide my erection. I climbed on my motorcycle and sped off, taking the hills on Leavenworth faster than normal. The wind in my face and not knowing what was over the hills as I accelerated gave me the life buzz. Knowing that a pothole, or an oil smudge, or an oncoming car could end my life in a breath made me laugh out loud. There was nothing reckless about it. I was more alert, my eyesight keener, my reactions quicker. If I were to die then, it would be God's doing and He'd have the last laugh. I suppose He always does.

When I got home I felt spent. I climbed in bed and again my thoughts turned toward Sarah.

It's funny how when someone you were close to is no longer in your life it's the inconsequential things that remain clear. Not the blow-outs, not the ecstasy, not the horrendous bloodletting, but the smell of the products she put in her hair, the way she made popcorn, the soft blond hair under her arms.

My last thought before floating off to sleep was of the way she would take a bath. Sitting in the steaming hot water with her back on the porcelain, her long legs out-stretched and extended toward the faucet, she would raise her feet and let a slow stream of cold water fall on to the top of her toes. The flow was barely more than a trickle. Taking her time she would go from toe to toe. She would smile, breathe deeply, then close her eyes. Sometimes she would giggle. It was private and it was beautiful. I would often spy on her through the door opening. She would have one candle lit, sitting in its holder on the sink. It would cast a shadow of her feet and ankles inside the bathtub. I never loved her more than in those moments.

Chapter 13

It rained the day I learned my mother was sick. I got up late as usual. I looked out the window and noticed that the streets were wet. Somehow it didn't register as rain. I was still half asleep and with the last few days of a January heat wave, I shrugged it off as the morning fog. I have a special motorcycle get-up I wear when it rains: black nylon ski pants I put on over my jeans, a pair of water-repellent ski gloves, a scarf, and a slicker I wear over a layer of shirts. I had no clue where any of those things were. I'd be fine. Besides it was probably sunny just over the hill.

I drove extra careful to work. The roads were slippery and the drivers were stupid. No zigzagging, no speeding. I was braking halfway down the hills. About halfway there, on the corner of Stockton and California, it started pouring sheets. I was cursing under my black helmet. When I finally got to work I was soaked. As I climbed off the Honda my jeans were plastered to my legs.

The rain had saturated my leather gloves. I had worn

my motorcycle jacket with the broken zipper. My chest and neck were cold and dripping.

By the time I walked into the studios it was 9:20. I had 9:30 headlines. I didn't have time to go online, print out the Reuters news, then rewrite. I'd have to read the wire copy cold.

I hate the way wire service reporters write. Their copy is always too wordy. They use five words when they could get by with two. And they're always using verbs and adjectives that I'd never use like "sealing" and "toppled." I always stumble on wire copy especially if I don't have time to prepare.

I printed out national and international news briefs with four minutes to spare. I decided I would record the newscast. I could always do a few takes if I screwed up. For some reason I was feeling frantic and scattered, best not to read the wire copy cold and live:

"THREE. TWO. ONE. HEADLINES FROM UNITED NEWS SERVICE. . . U.S. SECRETARY OF STATE MADELINE ALBRIGHT SAID TODAY THAT PRESIDENT CLINTON HAS APPROVED PEACE PLANS FOR BOSNIA'S ETHNIC RIVALS TO INSURE THE DIFFICULT PEACE PROCESS SUCCEEDS.

"THE FIRST WAR CRIMES TRIBUNAL IN GERMANY SINCE THE NUREMBERG NAZI TRIALS TOOK PLACE MORE THAN FIFTY YEARS AGO HAS ENDED IN A CONVICTION. GERMAN FEDERAL PROSECUTORS TOOK THE CASE DUE TO AN OVERLOAD IN THE HAGUE.

"TROOPS LOYAL TO LAURANT KABILA FIRED INTO THE AIR TODAY IN KINSHASA TO BREAK UP A PROTEST BY SUPPORTERS OF VETERAN

POPULIST POLITICIAN ILSO. . . OY—Fuck! What the fuck. . . ! fucking. . . kind of fucked name is that?

"Take two in. THREE. TWO. AND ONE. HEADLINES FROM UNITED NEWS SERVICE. RUSSIAN PRESI-DENT BORIS YELTSIN HAS CONFIRMED AS NEW DEFENSE SECRETARY IGOR SERG-I-A—FUCK!"

The next take was perfect. Good thing. I had just thirty seconds to air time.

Around noon I called home and checked my messages. "Martin, this is your mother. I need to talk to you. Call me when you get in."

It was strange and it was cold. The cold part didn't sur-prise me. She was still upset with me for not spending much time with her when I went down for Christmas. I was usually only in L.A. for a few days and I spread myself thin, visiting friends and family. Most of my time was spent on freeways. My divorced parents lived in the Valley, my sister lived in Santa Monica, my grandmother in Orange County, and my friends were spread out from Pasadena to Thousand Oaks. Most often I spent the night at my father's. It was the most comfortable and it was close to the airport. At least that's what I told myself and my mother. The truth is I had a difficult time spending more than a few hours with her.

When I went to visit, I'd get there late. We'd talk about a number of things including our careers and personal lives. She would always have an exceptional meal waiting. We'd eat, and then I'd feel the urge to leave. I admired my moth-er. We had a lot in common.

We both held the same political views. I was proud of her. She had gone back to school in her thirties, struggling to keep her grades up while raising two kids and surviving on college loans and Welfare. She was a dual major: psychology and Latin studies. She graduated with honors, earned her Ph.D., and was certified a clinical psychologist after she passed her state licensing exams, making her a Marriage, Family, Child Counselor. Before establishing her private practice she worked at a number of not-so-lucrative jobs. She was a forensic psychologist for the state, assessing the sanity of child molesters, rapists, and murderers. She was a counselor for Planned Parenthood. She was a student counselor at a variety of junior colleges before accepting a position at the state college she had graduated from. During her time there she established the nation's first date rape crisis center. She worked with people whose first language was Spanish as well as Vietnam vets and victims of domestic abuse. She was compassionate and caring in her work, but a hardness and bitterness compelled her. All the issues she dealt with were part of her own personal history. She worked hard and reached out to the people she treated and advised.

Through it all she became a role model for many young women. When she became too sick to take her own phone calls, women from all walks of life that had been her friends and clients called regularly. But no one understood her the way I did. Her career was really about discovering what made her the way she was, why she could be so hateful and bitter. Why she found it nearly impossible to love without violence. Why she beat the fuck out of her kids. Why the fuck did she beat her children? It haunted and tormented her. No matter how much good work she did for others, no matter how many emotional lives she had saved, no matter how many women thought of her as their "hero," she couldn't shake it. In the last years of her life she explored what she perceived to be an evil inside. On many occasions she tried to discuss the abuse with me. I would see the regret and sadness in her eyes as she tried to talk with me about it. At any hint of that regret or of an impending confession, I would bolt. I may as well have been in another body, or on another planet, or in the closet sleeping on my toy box. The only time my will could overpower my mother's was when my complete, my enveloping, my thoroughly necessary denial kept her at bay.

She'd recognize it—after all, she was a professional—and she'd back off. All she could say was, "Marty, maybe you should see a counselor. Just for maintenance. Even healthy people have shrinks."

I'd smile and say, "Yeah, maybe someday, Mom." But inwardly I vowed never to go. Even in the last few weeks before her death when the lucid moments came sparingly, she would bring up my childhood. "Marty, when you were a kid I did some things I shouldn't ha—"

I'd stroke her bald head through her scarf and cut her off, "No regrets, Mother. You made some mistakes. Everyone does. But I'm lucky to have had a mother like you."

"You really think so?"

"Absolutely! You taught me what was important. Go to sleep."

She nodded placidly and smiled. My words had comforted her but she was not at peace with those long past days. Perhaps that was her punishment, to go to her death still harboring guilt, seeing how utterly impossible it was for me to look directly at those times with honesty.

But I was good. Any time, with nearly all the women in my life, I could turn it on. But like most of those women, my dying mother sensed the desperation and transitoriness of my seduction. And like the others she gave me the benefit of the doubt because of the affection. The affection of a seven-year-old boy—scared and doubtful but reaching down to hold on to the illusion of tenderness.

I never caught up at work. All day long I was writing and rewriting. It was a busy news day with stories breaking late. Despite the uneasy feeling I had when I heard my mother's message, I didn't call her until I got home from work.

"Is this my son?"

"You know it's me. Is there something wrong?"

"I've been sick for a while. At first they thought it was pneumonia but now the doctor says it might be cancer."

"What?"

"It doesn't look good. The doctors want to do more tests. Marty, I'm scared."

"What did the doctor say exactly?"

"He showed me an x-ray. There's a number of spots on my lungs, and—" she started crying, "and they want me to, they want me to—oh, Marty, I think I have cancer!"

"Did the doctor say that you have cancer?"

"No. They want to do a biopsy and—"

"Then you don't know for sure if it's cancer?"

"No, but—"

"Listen to me, Mom. We don't know yet if it's cancer, so try not to get worked up. Take it a step at a time. If it is cancer we'll deal with it. Do you understand?"

"Can you come down?"

"When's the biopsy?"

"Tomorrow."

"What time?"

"Two o'clock."

"Good. I'll take a morning flight. I'll book it tonight then I'll call you back."

"Can you stay for a while?"

"We'll see."

She started crying again. "I don't want to die, Marty."

"What are you talking about? You're not going to die! If it is cancer then we'll fight it. Remember when they found that lump in your breast when I was a kid? You survived.

You have to get out of this frame of mind right now. Understand? You are going to live for a very long time. Say it."

Through the tears she responded, "I'm not going to die."

"No! Say, 'I'm going to live a very long life.' And stop crying."

"I'm going to live a very long life." Her voice was weak.

"Say it again, like you mean it!"

"I'M GOING TO LIVE A VERY LONG LIFE!"

"Goddamn right you are! I'll call you right back with the flight number."

I was putting death on notice. *Better not fuck with me, or I'll beat the shit out of you. I'll pounce and use everything I can to defeat you.*

What a joke.

She picked me up from the airport and asked me to drive home. She explained that the doctor told her that the procedure was actually minor surgery and that she'd have to spend the night in the hospital. They were going in to take a bit of her infected lung and scope her insides. There was a sense of doom in the car. I tried to make conversation about work and I asked her how my sister and her two kids were. She brightened up when she started talking about her grandchildren, Louie and Jimmy. Louie was two and Jimmy was just six months old. "Little Louie knows his grandma."

"Of course he does."

"I took him to the petting zoo on Parthenia last week. You should have seen him. He has your sister's eyes, big and round. He's going to be a smart one," she said, choking back tears.

"I know this is hard, Mom, but we've got to be strong. Your attitude is going to be very important if we are going to fight. Until we know for sure one way or the other, I think you should try not to think about it. Did the doctor say when they'll have the results?"

"He said they should have an idea right after the biopsy, but they won't know for sure until Monday."

"Who's the doctor?"

"Dr. Thompkins. He's the specialist doing the biopsy. Dr. Blair recommended him." Dr. Blair had been our family doctor for as long as I could remember. He had set my broken arm I got playing football when I was eleven. He was there for other maladies and catastrophes over the years. He was a good old general practitioner, a dying breed. We trusted him completely. He had a son my age.

"Is Dr. Blair going to be there?"

"No. He's turned everything over to Dr. Thompkins and an oncologist named Dr. Allen."

We drove to her condo in the valley. She packed and I ate. "There's tamales in the freezer."

"From Christmas?"

"I just haven't gotten around to eating them. I haven't had much of an appetite lately."

I ate six tamales and cleaned up the kitchen. Then we drove to the hospital.

I had always liked hospitals. At first I thought my attraction to the sterile environment, the smell of disinfectant, the white and powder blue worn by hospital personnel was abnormal and somehow repulsive.

When I was twelve my friend Jay Hemmlestien's mother had been in a bad car accident. She had a fractured skull, three broken ribs, a broken arm, and a ruptured spleen.

It was touch and go for awhile. I was antsy when I went to visit her the first time. Jay interpreted it as an aversion to hospitals and a natural sympathy for his mother, and I went along. But it was more of a nervous excitement, like a first date with someone you've had your eye on for a while. I was at the hospital constantly during her two week stay.

When I wasn't in her room I was wandering the halls and various wards. When I was on a floor I shouldn't have been on, the desk nurses would ask if they could help me. I'd answer with "Is the trauma ward on this floor?"

In the hospital I could sense and feel death's presence. It was as near as that girl's pussy at the Lusty Lady. I wondered where the morgue was. As I wandered the halls I would look at each nurse, each doctor, each orderly and ask myself, *I wonder if that person has seen a dead body today?*

My grandfather died when I was eight and an uncle was killed in jail, but death was still abstract to me, a mystery to be discovered. Movies and books and the news had sufficed for most of my youth, but it paled compared to the perceptible, tangible, savory feel of death I had in the hospital.

As a young reporter in Santa Barbara I craved the police beat. I wore the ghoulish and macabre like booty. I'd go to work and hope to cover something violent: a murder, a fire, a horrible car crash, a police shoot-out. One time I walked into the newsroom and my news director told me there was a double homicide at a motel in Goleta. He'd heard the call on the scanner. Did I want to go? "I might miss my noon newscast."

"That's alright. I'll cover for you."

"Thanks John, I owe you." I was the first reporter on the scene, showing up just after the squad cars but before the detectives. The door of the cheap motel room where the victims had lived—a born again Christian couple—was open. The officers would not let me in, but I could see the crime scene.

Two naked bodies lay on the floor with their hands tied behind their backs. There was blood splattered on the couch not two feet from their heads. The man's body was facedown. His head was half gone, a mass of tangled brown hair and blood in the crater that had been his skull. Gray duct tape was wrapped around his neck, presumably circling over his mouth. A small pool of blood and black shit had gathered between his pale white legs.

The woman was more on her side with her legs huddled up around her waist. There was blood caked down both legs. The upturned part of her face was black with blood. There was a large hole where her right eye used to be. Her mouth was forced shut but the bloodied tape did not extend around her neck or the back of her head. They had both been sodomized, then shot point blank. It was my first murder scene and it was nothing like *Columbo*. I caught little more than a glimpse before being turned away by the officer at the door.

I remember wanting to see more. I felt the need to study the grizzly details: every piece of brain, the direction of the blood flow, the color and indentations of the shit, the dirty soles of their feet, the thickness of the rope that held their rigid hands tied, the lack of hair on the male victim's arms, the matted blonde and bloodied mane of the female, the cellulite on her buttocks and thighs, the way the duct tape crumpled around the man's neck. I always thought of myself as more or less a big picture kind of person, never good with details. But with these deaths, I realized it was the *details* that gave the whole its epiphany. Emotions burst to the surface. The horror dredged up something familiar, but evasive. Death had never been so pulsating, yet so still. I wanted to turn away but I couldn't. I felt that if I were to walk through the threshold into that stench filled death scene I would have been swallowed by something utterly unexplainable, perhaps a moment of so-called enlightenment.

As I took out my notebook and began writing the story,

I sucked those feelings into the vast pit of my subconscious. Whatever emotions I was having, they were unacceptable. I convinced myself that it was the job, the pressure of reporting, the immediacy of what had happened, the rush to beat my competitors, that was pumping the adrenaline. It was my first real taste of death. It had excited me. Captured me. My heart had practically pounded through my shirt, my hands were sweaty, my senses thrilled.

It felt like love.

They came and took my mother from her hospital room just after 2:00. I was told it would be about an hour and that the doctor would look for me in the waiting room once the procedure was completed. I left the hospital, got into my mother's white Toyota, and drove to a nearby Mexican restaurant. I sat and read the paper while eating huevos rancheros. The Lakers were on a winning streak heading into the playoffs.

I returned to the hospital about 3:00 and went into the waiting room. Half hour later Dr. Thompkins came out. He was in his operating garb. He looked around the waiting room, then we made eye contact. "Martin?"

"Dr. Thompkins?"

"Come with me."

We walked down the corridor to a spot near the gift shop. He didn't say much. Strangely and suddenly I didn't want to know much, as if the less he said the better our chances would be. "It's not good. She has a mass of lung tissue that is engulfed." He looked me squarely in the eyes with an apprehension that seemed like sadness. I almost let myself feel compassion for him, but I didn't. He told me that the official results would be reviewed with my mother and me on Monday at Dr. Allen's office and that Dr. Allen would plan out a strategy for fighting the cancer. There was no hope in his voice. I thanked him and then he walked out of our lives forever.

"You have advance adenocarcinoma, a nonsmall cell lung cancer. I say it's advanced because an infinite number of cancer cells have spread, or metastasized outside the lung to other areas." Dr. Allen would be our main doctor from now on.

"What other areas?" I asked.

"The bronchial tubes, nearby lymph nodes, and the right lung. Perhaps to the bones and brain. We'll have to take more tests to make sure."

My mother couldn't speak. She sat there with her hand clenched around mine, under the chair. "'To make sure?'" I asked. "You sound as if it's a done deal?"

"I'm sorry, Laura, but at this stage it's likely that the cancer has metastasized to other parts of your body that we have not yet detected. Normally in lung cancer it's in the brain and bones."

"Can you remove the lung?" I asked.

"No. It's inoperable—"

"You said that before. What does that mean, and why can't you take out the infected lung?"

"The cancer has spread to a portion of the other lung, a small portion, but nonetheless a portion. If we were to remove all the infected areas there wouldn't be enough lung capacity to breathe. Also, removing the lung wouldn't cure the cancer. This type of cancer moves fast. I think the sooner we begin treatment, the better."

"Why don't you know if it's spread to the brain and the bones yet?"

"The biopsy Dr. Thompkins performed was for the lung area only. We needed to know quickly if what we saw on the x-rays were indeed malignant cancer cells so we could formulate a treatment plan as soon as possible."

"So now you know. Have you formed your strategy yet?"

"Well, that's one of the reasons we're here today."

He turned toward my mother and leaned a bit over his desk to address her directly. "Laura, it's very important that we begin treatment right away.

"We're going to have to do a CT scan to determine if the cancer has spread to your brain. Also we'll have to do a bone marrow biopsy. In the meantime I'd like to schedule radiation treatment right away. After the radiation, which will take about three weeks, I want you to undergo chemotherapy."

"Why both?" I questioned.

"The radiation will be used to damage the cancer cells in your lungs," he was still looking directly at my mother, "and hopefully get them to stop spreading so fast. The chemotherapy, which we'll administer intravenously in my office, will be used to kill cancer cells throughout your body."

"Wait a minute. Isn't chemotherapy toxic? I think we should get a second opinion. No offense, doctor."

"None taken, Martin."

"No, Marty, I trust Dr. Allen."

"It's not a matter of trust, Mom. It's a good idea to get a second opinion, Isn't that right, Doctor?"

"I can give you the test results, along with my findings and observations, and I can recommend another doctor for you, or if you have someone in mind?"

"No, Marty. Let's just continue with Doctor Allen."

"Mom, we're talking about your life here!"

"I just want to get on with it." Then she paused before asking, "How long do I have to live, Doctor?"

"I can't really say."

"How long do people usually live in my condition, Dr. Allen?"

"With the right treatment I've seen patients survive a year." He said it as if we understood that she'd be dead a lot sooner. Her hand went limp in mine. She had accepted her death sentence. I grabbed it tightly as if attempting to wake her from a dream: *Wake up damn it! We're not going without a fight!*

A week later the doctor informed us that the cancer had metastasized to her brain and bones.

CHAPTER 14

"Come this way, dear." The radiation therapy nurse, Linda, motioned for my mother.

"Can my son come in with me?"

"Sure."

We walked into the treatment room. It was cold. The tile floor was white and in the corner of the room was an area where the patient could change into a hospital gown. The bright florescent lights were giving me a headache. In the middle of room sat what my mother called the "White Monster." The Linear Accelerator was an imposing multi angled machine that delivered beams tens of thousands of times more powerful than used to produce a common chest x-ray. My mother changed into her gown. She was then told to lie down on the treatment table, which was in the back of the room to the right. Linda left and told us that the radiation therapist, would join us shortly. A few minutes later, Dr. Teller, a short, stout woman with medium-length red hair and narrow gray eyes, entered. She was pleasant and direct.

She explained that the gamma rays would be directed at my mother's left lung and surrounding area would hopefully stop the rapid spread of the cancer cells, but there were no guarantees. I was asked to leave the room, at which time the doctor asked my mother to take off her gown.

Mother was outfitted with a plaster mold that had been designed for the contours of her upper body. An area was left open in the mold, where the rays would zap the cancer cells. I waited for the doctor outside the treatment room. She came out and motioned for me to follow. We went into a small, cramped room, which looked like a TV control booth with a monitor, along with a number of other instruments, and what looked like a control board. On the screen was the image of my mother, looking ridiculous in her plaster cast, lying on the treatment table. The doctor pushed a few buttons and the White Monster went to work. It made a steady buzzing sound as the gamma rays beamed into my mother's chest. I thought of the transporter in *Star Trek*. *Beam me up, Scotty*. Beam me up out of this surreal joke. The role I've waited my entire life to play: caretaker to a dying mother. Beam me up and beam out those abnormal, metastasized, wild, bone-eating, brain-sucking, lung-chewing, breath-stealing, adenocarcinoma, nonsmall cancer cells.

Three weeks of radiation, twice a week, didn't help. Through the skin rashes, through the dryness, through the fatigue, through the loss of appetite, through the vaginal drying, through the sluggish bowels, through the thickened saliva and dry mouth, those goddamned little cancer cells kept multiplying, billions everyday breaking off and crowding out healthy, normal cells.

No technology, no supercomputer could distinguish the microscopic killers advancing into various parts of my mother's innards: the upper, middle, and lower lobes of her left lung, the upper lobe of her right, the inside of her trachea, the outer lining of her esophagus, the outside of her ascending aorta. Not only was the cancer attacking the areas around her heart, but it was also making its assault on her brain: the corpus callosum, her skull bone, and her cerebrum. An infinite number of cancer cells. Like the expanding universe there was no end. The lively little bastards were evil in their ignorance, knowing only to split and spread, and grow and move, having no consciousness that soon their host would cease to function as life and with that would come their demise. The infinite would become nothing.

I was there for each treatment, sitting in the control room with Dr. Teller as she manipulated the soft red beam of the Linear Accelerator. With each successive treatment the scene became more comedic. My mother being automatically turned upward at a forty-five-degree angle on the treatment bed, her upper body covered with white plaster, her lower body shielded with thick gray anti-gamma ray mats. Her normally dark brown face pale and still. She looked like an albino Grace Jones.

"Okay, doc, zap the motherfuckers," she would say.

After one of her final treatments, upon returning home, I made her some salt-free chicken broth and wheat toast with honey. She ate only a small amount. Before falling asleep she asked if I could look for the terms of her insurance. She was worried about having to have a home nurse.

As I searched through the modest desk in her small office I discovered a black leather-bound work journal. Under normal circumstances I wouldn't have read it:

October 18th, 1992

Re: Roberto Garza

Abuse issues finally starting to surface. However, may have to refer client to another therapist despite continued progress.

Major breakthrough: Roberto broke down and cried uncontrollably while relating memories of repeated attacks by neighborhood boys. Beginning to open up about his abusive youth as both victim and abuser. Vivid recollection of previously repressed memories. Had to reel him in, slow down process for fear of overload. Anger remaining strong but grief and sadness starting to be verbalized.

While he was relating story of molestation of younger sister as a boy, I was overcome with memories of my older brother. My professional and human concern turned to hatred, which surprised and upset me. I indicated no outward emotion, however inside I was outraged and at one point thought, "You bastard. You should be dead." Can't go there. Memories of demon child tying me up, beating me, locking me in dark spaces coming up at inappropriate moments.

Damn him! I will not allow that. Will not let him affect my practice.

Will explore with David on Tuesday.

CHAPTER 15

"It's late son, time for bed."

"Ah, Mom!"

"I'm going to bed too. You want to sleep with me tonight?"

"Okay."

"I'll tell you what. You can stay up and watch TV for as long as it takes me to clean up and get ready for bed. Deal?"

"Deal."

Martin's mother walked down the hall into her bedroom. She opened her closet door and stood in front of the full-length mirror. She thought the mirror made her look thinner than she was. Not that she needed to be thinner. She was a scant 105 pounds. But now she was three months pregnant and wondered if she was beginning to show. She stripped and examined herself. She had heard that women let themselves go in the second pregnancy and she was determined not to let that happen. As she eyed herself up close in the mirror she reached up and grasped her firm, small breasts. *They're a bit larger*, she thought. *I like them.*

She gripped with satisfaction, then gently fingered her nipples. She put her palms on each areola, spreading her fingers. Her middle fingertips interlocked. She let her hands move slowly from her body, just far enough away so that her fingertips were circling her nipples. She started squeezing lightly then tugging gently. They were soon hard. She looked at her eyes and her long, black Mexican hair, which was parted in the middle and caressed each shoulder. She whispered aloud to the mirror, *You're beautiful, Laura. Tu bonita, Laurita.* Her eyes drifted downward where the sight of her thick mound elevated her arousal. She surveyed the entire package: her thin, strong legs, her small, perfectly proportioned feet (size 5), the dark, soft hair on her arms, her long fingers and painted nails, her round hips. *Not an ounce of fat. Three months pregnant and not an ounce of fat.* She let her left hand move down her belly while continuing to rub her breasts with her right. She began twirling her pubic hair in her fingers. She pressed down and noticed her lips had swelled. She felt a wetness in her vagina. She spread herself with her forefinger and ring finger and reached up with her middle finger to feel the wetness.

She brought the finger up and began teasing her clitoris. She moved slow at first and then touching herself like no man ever could, she brought herself to orgasm.

"Marty, come to bed now!"

Martin went to the bathroom and brushed his teeth. He went into his room and put on his pajama bottoms and a T-shirt. The only pajamas he had were flannel. It was late August and Los Angeles was in the middle of a heat wave. He turned off the lights and walked down the short and narrow hallway to his mother's bedroom. She heard him enter the room and when she spoke it startled him. His eyes had not become acclimated to the darkness.

"Come to bed, Marty."

"I'm coming." He crawled under the white sheets.

Laura had turned down the thick, brown-patterned bedspread to the foot of the queen-sized bed. Martin was tired. He moved up next to his mother and lay on his back, his head on one of her many pillows.

"Do you want to cuddle, Marty?" He hesitated. "Please? Your mother needs you to cuddle, Marty."

He moved closer and put his head on her shoulder and wrapped his right arm around her upper body. She wore only a T-shirt. Moments later she began stroking his hair. "You're such a beautiful little boy Marty. Thank you for standing by me. Everything's going to be all right, you know? It'll be a beautiful baby, just like you were."

"I'm not a little boy, Mom."

"I suppose you're not. You're getting to be quite a little man." She felt sweat on his forehead. "It's awfully hot to be wearing those pajamas isn't it?"

"I'm okay."

"Why don't you take them off?"

"I'm fine."

"Marty, you're sweating. At least take off your T-shirt."

Without getting up he pulled the shirt over his head and threw it on the floor. "That's better," his mother said.

He started drifting off to sleep when Laura asked, "Are you sleeping, Marty?"

"No."

"I was just thinking. You were such a cute little baby. Right after you were potty trained, you used to get so excited about being able to go to the bathroom by yourself. I'd be watching TV or making dinner and I'd hear you yell from the bathroom while you were sitting on the pot,

'Mom, it's hard.' You remember that?"

"No."

"You were so cute, mijo. Do you still get hard like that?"

"I don't know."

"It's natural. It happens to all boys and men. Does it happen to you a lot?"

"Sometimes."

"How does it feel?"

"I want it to go away. It's uncomfortable."

"Do you ever touch it?"

"No, well, sometimes when I'm in the car or on the bus, I put my hand in my pocket and push it down so no one will see it."

"It feels good to touch it, or massage it with no clothes on. You want to try it?"

"I don't know. Besides, it's not hard."

"Do you think we could make it hard?"

"I think so."

"Lie back, sweetheart." She reached over and put her hand in the opening of his pajamas. She touched his soft, small penis gently with just her first two fingers.

In an instant it was hard and protruding through the flannel unrestricted. She gripped it and began massaging slowly. "Does that feel good, Marty?" she whispered.

"Yes." He'd never felt anything like it.

At that moment, neither one felt any guilt or shame. The boy had yet to learn that this was "wrong." He had no conscious concept of sexuality: what was appropriate and what wasn't. He trusted his mother. The steady movement was both relaxing and pleasurable.

Laura had convinced herself that it was not sexual. She was helping to relax her son. It brought him pleasure, she sensed that. She also knew he was wise beyond his years and that he would have stopped her if he didn't feel it was okay. Society be damned! She loved her son. She was bringing him some pleasure.

There was nothing wrong with that. For God's sake, she wasn't going to rape the boy! It would never go beyond a massage. She refused to feel guilt. Years later she would feel quite differently. In therapy she would break down and sob, reliving how she had "taken advantage" of her poor little boy. But at that moment, while she masturbated her prepubescent son, she felt no regret, despite her awareness that what she was doing could be interpreted as bad.

Throughout the pregnancy, the abuse continued. But it progressed. Progressed to things that the older Marty buried deep to that place in his memory that was inaccessible.

CHAPTER 16

Sex is my shepherd, I shall not want (for sex).
Sex maketh me to lie down in green pastures: Sex lead-
eth me besides still waters.
Sex restoreth my soul: Sex leadeth me in the path of
righteousness for sex's sake.
Yea though I walk through the
valley of the shadow of death,
I will fear no sex:
Thy sex and thy staff they comfort me.
Sex preparist a table before me in
the presence of mine enemies:
Thou annointest my head with oil:
My sex runneth over.
Surely sex shall follow me all the days of my life and I
will dwell in the house of the Lord forever.

She was rarely herself during and after the chemotherapy. We'd sit in Doctor Allen's office for hours while they pumped a combination of cancer-killing drugs into her compromised system. They hooked up an IV into her arm and the external pump fed her bloodstream with unnerving silence. The Cisplatin and Doxorubicin were also killing a number of healthy cells, but we didn't talk about that. Before the first treatment the doctor gave my mother a list of side effects.

It looked something like this: *Nausea and vomiting, red urine (usually lasts one day after each dose), hair loss, loss of appetite, heart problems, diarrhea, numbness and tingling in fingers, toes and, or face. You need to take antinausea medicine for the first 24 hours and for the following four days. You need to take extra liquids to prevent kidney problems.*

Those were the "common" side effects. The "occasional" side effects included: *Dizziness, loss of taste, blurred vision, change in ability to see colors, difficulty in hearing, ringing in ears, sores in mouth, fast heartbeat or wheezing, fever, chills and sore throat, decreased urination, swelling of feet or lower legs, unusual bleeding or bruising, darkening of soles, shortness of breath, pain in joints, side or stomach, burning pain at injection site.*

Along with her motor skills went her hair. In recent years she had let it grow beyond the small of her back. She had also stopped coloring. It was about a third gray. The contrast of her thick as thread black mane combined with the white hairs added to her regal mystery. At fifty, people were still taken aback by her beauty.

She mourned the loss of her hair like the death of a child, crying for days. I tried to comfort her by saying it was a unique fashion and not too many people could pull off the "bald lady look." We bought hats and scarfs. For a while she wore a funky, flimsy, black velvet top-hat-looking lid that had a petrified gardenia pinned to its front. Ultimately she settled on wearing a silk paisley scarf that one of her clients had given her as a gift.

As my mother's disease progressed, my father took it upon himself to comfort me in his own unique way, setting me up with a hot little hostess at the restaurant. "Paula wants to go out with you, and she's horny as hell."

"What? How do you know that?"

"She told me. We're friends. She tells me everything."

"And she told you she wants to go out with me? What exactly did she say?"

"What exactly did she say? I don't know, kid. Something like you're looking good and she wants to get it on with you."

"'Get it on' with me? You know you date yourself with that kind of talk, old man."

"Marvin Gaye, baby!"

"She actually said she wants to have sex with me?"

"I wouldn't be telling you otherwise. Here's her number. Give her a call, take your mind off things. Be careful, though. She likes it up the butt."

"Did she tell you *that* too?"

"Not in so many words. But you know me, kid. I understand human nature."

"Yeah, you and the Devil."

My father was always a better friend than a father. But that was his charm. I resented it for about two minutes when I was an adolescent, something about his not having been there when I was growing up. Complaining seemed the thing to do at the time.

But just like practically everyone who knew him, I came to accept the fact that I was happier when in his presence.

As a young man he played professional baseball but was released when his carousing began affecting his batting average. As a boy growing up on the streets of Brooklyn, he was pegged as the next Joe DiMaggio. He was signed out of high school by the then New York Giants, bitter rivals to his beloved Dodgers. In his first year he tore up the Carolina rookie league, leading the team in home runs and RBI's and finishing third in batting with a .321 average. But after three years on the road in the minors, drinking and fucking at every chance, the 6'1", green-eyed, olive-skinned, former altar boy began to burn out. His numbers dipped and even after attempting to walk the straight and narrow, he was cut one spring training after working out with the big club to make room for a left-handed pitcher.

Until he remarried in his late forties, he played it loose. Like the Three Stooges, over the years he held a variety of jobs, mostly provided by his never-ending supply of friends. He drove a cab for awhile and worked construction. He was an executive for a clothing manufacturer, a letter carrier, a furniture delivery man. But the "job" that he always looked back on with the most affection was the year he was unemployed and survived off his winnings at the race track. I remembered that time. He played a lot of golf and traveled with his softball team to tournaments throughout the west. It was back when softball was somewhat big and drew large crowds in smaller towns. The owner of his softball team was a lady's shoe magnate who was married to Debbie Reynolds. Debbie became a sort of team mother, hanging out with the players and providing show tickets when she performed in Vegas. A few years later I met her backstage after one of her performances. She was sweet, but I remember thinking, *What a horrible wig.*

My father did all right playing the ponies, losing his share but always a "nose" away from retirement. Now he was managing an Italian restaurant for a friend and taking football bets on the side for another friend. He worked like a mule at the restaurant but reveled in the human contact. It was his social and business ballpark. The old man had juice.

His customers included professional athletes, comedians, car mechanics, soap opera stars, various business owners, and the homeless. A pizza here, a chicken marsala there, parlayed into hockey tickets, Vegas shows, tires for his Nissan, dry cleaning, movie passes, golf clubs, a cellular phone, etc. Everyone knew him and all were charmed, except for a few of the waiters and waitresses whom he occasionally berated with a grin. "What are you, stupid? How many times do I have to tell you? Table five!" As he aged he started looking like a cross between Tommy Lasorda and Robert Mitchum. And like the actor, he loved to smoke pot.

After the biopsy, I had started camping out at my mother's condo. Sharon and Tom had agreed to let me take a leave of absence for as long as I needed. It was nice but unpaid. With my mother sick and not able to work her private practice, no money was coming in. We were living mostly off her savings. I sublet my apartment to a friend who had just moved down from Seattle, so that helped.

Whenever I could, I'd get away to the restaurant, where my father would feed me for free.

"How's your mother doing?"

"The same. She's in and out. One day she's alert, the next she's in a fog. She's not eating anything, getting weaker by the hour."

"Well, ask her if she wants some pot. Maybe it'll help her with the pain and get her appetite back a little."

"It's that damn chemotherapy! I told her it wasn't a good idea. So she lives an extra couple of months, maybe. At what price? It's knocking the piss out of her, Dad. She can barely get up to go to the bathroom, when she does go, every other week. Goddamned doctors! Give her this drug, give her that drug. Zap the fuck out of her!"

"Is she eating? You want to take something home?"

"That's another thing. Her diet! The doctor says to feed her just about anything—just to get her to eat. What kind of talk is that? Food is important. We need to regenerate her immune system, so we can fight back the cancer. I've looked into all sorts of shit. Meditation, chiropractic, alternative diets. This herbal stuff I have her on has really helped. I've got different capsules for different parts of her body. . . Maybe if the doctors encouraged her."

"Take it easy, kid. There's not much more you can do. You need to relax a bit. Take care of yourself. Give Paula a call."

"Maybe. Remember My Mother the Car?"

"Yeah?"

"We should start our own show: My Father the Pimp."

"You could do a lot worse. And you have."

The weeks dragged by like a dead whale being towed off the beach. As my mother became further incapacitated, the social calls and business of taking care of her financial matters increased to breakneck. I was her maid, her social secretary, her cook, her nurse, and her power of attorney.

She signed everything over to me. I did her taxes and paid her bills. Strange thing is that I was running her life with a precision and vigor I had never had for my own.

The last few months before her death my mother had visitors nonstop. Colleagues, present and past friends, distant and closely related family members were constantly calling and coming over. Every day my grandmother would call and ask if she should come and stay for good. "No, Grandma, not yet." I'd set up times for people to come and visit from morning until sunset. My mother enjoyed all the attention, when she was awake. I was doing all the things that in my own life I usually put off. Somehow I began enjoying the newfound power. Being in control of her life gave the illusion that I was in control of her death. When I would slow down, the reality of the situation would take hold. I couldn't accept that, so I fled into the carnal. The all consuming, forgiving, obsequious carnal, my one and only friend. The way to beat back death was to fuck.

"Paula?"

"Yes?"

"Hi, it's Martin."

"Where are you? It sounds like a party."

"No, I'm at the bar at Howard Johnson's."

"The one down the street on Ventura Boulevard?"

"No. Listen I know it's short notice, but would you like to get together after work? Maybe have a few drinks?"

"Sounds great. I'm closing up with your dad, but I should be done around ten-thirty."

"Good. I'll swing by then."

"Since you're so close you can come by now and eat before we close the kitchen. I'm sure your father would like to see you."

"No, thanks, I'm going to stay here and have a drink. I'll see you later." I was already drunk and was talking to a blonde at the bar who I hoped would provide her phone number for future reference.

Her name was Tammy and she had wonderfully pouty, pink lips. Sarah was never far from my thoughts though, and when I ordered my third bourbon and water I thought of her and her dead father. As I put the glass to my mouth and poured the liquor over my tongue, I tasted Sarah. As the bourbon made its way down my gullet into the part of my stomach that ached to be murdered, I heard her whisper, *Te quiero*.

Tammy gave me her phone number after reluctantly accepting that we wouldn't be spending any time together that night. "I don't usually ask a guy I just met to come home with me. Oh, it's probably better if you call anyway. That way I'll respect you in the morning. Ah, come on, just come back with me tonight."

She was drunk, which hadn't stopped me from going home with women in the past. But I was geared up for Paula. "I can't. . . really."

"Why not?"

"I have a date."

"Oh."

"But I'll call in a day or two."

I walked to the restaurant. I'd let Paula drive wherever we were going. She could chance the DUI. She smiled when she saw me enter through the front doors. "Hi. It's going to be another half hour or so before we close up. You want to eat something?"

"Yeah, all right. I'm going to the back and say 'hi' to the old man." I went to the back window where my father was working. He asked what I wanted to eat and I told him chicken sesame. He hollered to the cook to make it good. I went back out front and Paula directed me to an empty table. Between seating customers, helping serve, and taking phone calls, she would come and sit with me. She asked what I wanted to do. I suggested we go dancing. She agreed.

I ate. She and my father closed the restaurant, and we left.

"Can you drive?" I asked.

"Sure. Where did you have in mind?"

"How about the Strip?"

"The Sunset Strip?"

"Yeah. Does that sound all right?"

"Fine with me."

We ended up at a dance club called the Caribbean Zone. The building was painted a vibrant purple and red and had plastic palm tress surrounding the entrance (like there's a shortage of *real* palm trees in L.A.). Inside were four dance floors on three levels, all with their own motifs. We spent most of our time in the one that was decorated like a cave out of the Flintstones. Big, brown, Styrofoam rocks were scattered across the black-carpeted floor. To get there we had to descend a flight of stairs. In the corner of the dance floor was a DJ playing hard, driving music that pounded in my brain. After two drinks each I grabbed Paula and ran out onto the dance floor. We began gyrating to the heavy on the bass, drum, and trumpet music.

I teased her, grinding my erection against her leg while glaring into her loose, gray eyes. She began looking more attractive to me, with her small frame and light brown, medium length hair that was getting sweatier by the minute. As I stared into those blow-job eyes, it was as if we were alone in some dark, mystic place. I would not look away. Every second my gaze became more intense, bearing into her like a drill bit. I wanted to fuck her immediately, but I waited. She reached down and grabbed me through my pants and grimaced. *You may have me, but I've got you,* said her vampire stare. I grabbed her hair and brought her mouth an inch from my lips, then I twirled on the dance floor and laughed.

As we entered the motel on Ventura Boulevard, the door closed and our clothes came off. I laid her face-up on the edge of the bed next to the mahogany dresser and mounted her enthusiastically. She wrapped her thin legs around my lower back and we went at it. The light was on. As we pounded, my knee knocked open the bottom drawer of the dresser.

Out fell a Bible. "Do you believe in God?" I asked her. "Without a doubt."

"Do you believe He's here with us now?"

"Yes I do. But He's not alone."

"No?" I was curious.

"The Angel of Darkness is here as well."

"*I'm* the Angel of Darkness. Do you ever read the Bible?"

"Not in years."

"What's your favorite part?"

"I don't remember."

"The Sermon on the Mount is mine. Read it to me." I handed her the black King James version.

"Now?"

"There's no time like the present." She quickly turned the onion-skin pages. "It's Matthew, chapter five."

I flipped her onto her stomach. Her breasts and belly were on the bed with her head arched up. Her feet were on the floor. As she began reading, I started caressing the small of her back and her smooth, white ass. *"And seeing the multitudes, he went up into a mountain: and when he was set, his disciples came unto him."*

I moved in between her legs and put my penis up against her asshole. She sighed. "Don't stop reading," I whispered.

"And he opened his mouth, and taught them, saying." And I pushed the head of my penis into her rectum. "Uhhh!" she moaned. Then she continued reading. *"Blessed are the poor in spirit: for theirs is the kingdom of heaven."* And I forced all of my penis up inside her.

"Ayyy!" she cried out as she continued reading. *"Blessed are they that mourn: for they are comforted."* And I withdrew slowly.

"Blessed are the meek: for they shall inherit the earth." And I thrust forcefully back up inside her.

"Ahhh!" she screamed, and her breaths became quicker and her voice began to quiver. *"Blessed are they which hunger and thirst after righteousness: for they shall be filled!"* And I thrust again while shouting, "And what about mercy!?"

And she continued. *"Blessed are the merciful: for they— uh-uh!—shall obtain mercy!"*

And I thrust again and moaned, "What about war?"

And she cried out, *"BLESSED ARE THE PEACE-MAKERS: FOR THEY SHALL BE CALLED THE CHILDREN OF GOD!"*

I picked up the pace and rhythm and with each breath she would grunt. "And what about the fucking righteous?" I demanded. *"BLESSED ARE—uhh! . . . uhh! . . . oh God!— THEY WHICH ARE PERSE—ah! . . . ah!—CUTED FOR RIGHTEOUSNESS SAKE: FOR THEIRS IS THE KING-DOM OF—oh fuck! . . . uhh, uhh, uhh—HEAVEN."*

As she reached down and began fingering herself with one hand she held down the book with the other and continued reading with a flurry of pain and urgency that would have exorcised the demon out of any sinner. *"BLESSED-ARE-YE-WHEN-MEN-SHALL-REV-VILE-YOU!, AND-PER-SE-CUTE-YOU!, AND-SHALL-SAY-ALL-MAN-NER-OF-EVIL-AGAINST-YOU-FOR-MY-SAKE. REJOICE! AND-BE-EXCEEDINGLY-GLAD!: FOR-GREAT-IS-YOUR-REWARD-IN-HEAVEN—AND* INSIDE ME. . . AND FUCKING ME! . . . Yes! Yes! Keep fucking me! Keep fucking! Fucking! Fucking! Fucking! Yes! Yes! Yes! . . . YES!!" And she let out a piercing scream that

echoed throughout the motel parking lot. "AHHHH!"
Then we fell in a heap on the bed.

CHAPTER 17

"You're hurting her! Give me that! I'll do it."

"We need to do this. She can't breathe."

"Fucking right she can't breathe and you're not making it any easier! You're hurting her, Goddamn it!"

"Listen, I'm sorry for yelling. Really, I think I can do it best. Please let me do it. It can't hurt, right?"

"Well, you can try, but I'm doing the best I can." She gave me an *I'm the professional here, I know what I'm doing* look and reluctantly handed over the straw like plastic tube that was attached to a small vacuum. I thanked the little, fat nurse, whom I would much rather have thrown out the window, and eased the tube down my mother's throat.

I had become quite proficient at the suctioning task. I'd gotten a lot of practice the last few days. The other nurses understood, but this one was new. Mom was on a morphine drip, and every now and then she would flash a look of recognition. Recognition of me, or a visitor, or my grandmother, or her situation.

The cancer was interfering with the flow of air through her breathing tube making her wheeze every time she took a breath. The tumor, now the size of a softball, was making her cough all the time. The normal upward flow of mucus was being obstructed and gathering in her bronchus. In her condition, there was no way for her to cough it out, so it had to be removed for her.

I turned up the suction on the machine with one hand and rubbed her forehead with the other. Whenever the nurses tried, my mother's eyes would widen and a look of dismay would form on her skeletal face. She was drugged out but she knew something was up and she would struggle. The nurses would fight with her at first. Initially, she would react the same with me. But once she sensed my touch, she would relax and I could get far enough down to give her some relief. Then she would sleep.

She was in the hospital only temporarily. The doctor suggested she be checked in to give me a break. However, I insisted she return home at some point. I would not allow her to die in the hospital.

As a child she made me promise to never "put her away." She was obsessed with the thought of dying in a nursing home. "We have to take care of each other, Marty. Promise me you'll never put me away."

"Don't be silly."

"Marty. Please promise me you'll never put me away to die!"

So I decided not to take any chances when she got sick.

That stay in the hospital lasted a week. It was the week the Rodney King riots broke out in Los Angeles. I would spend most of the day in her hospital room, reading to her, hosting visitors, and watching TV. There was a curfew on, even in the Valley. I sat and watched the riots unfold on the television suspended above my mother's bed. I watched as black men destroyed their own neighborhoods. I watched as black teenagers threw rocks through windows of Korean-owned liquor stores, looting and beating anyone who crossed their path and setting fire to anything they could find as fuel.

I watched as a truck driver was unceremoniously hauled from his cab by a gang of black toughs who beat him senseless, kicking him and bludgeoning him with a brick. I watched as the smoke and fire and pandemonium engulfed the City of Angels, my hometown but no longer my home. Living in San Francisco I had felt far removed from Los Angeles. I had disowned the city of my birth, fleeing from the smog, and the traffic, and the sprawl. Running from the failure of my youth. Bolting from the scene of crimes both perpetrated against and by me. Going to L.A. had become a chore.

Family and friends and sometimes work brought me back, but oh, how glad I was to return home to my adopted city of misfits and fuck-ups, of hills and magical staircases that led to enchanted and sometimes spectacular vistas, of water and fog and disenfranchised Asian whores. But sitting in the hospital room watching Los Angeles go up in flames, a surprising nostalgia and kinship overcame me. Hour after hour sitting with my mother, day after day watching LArmageddon, oddly enough I didn't feel the frantic, choking urge to flee, to run from the two things I had run from my entire life.

As she lay there, escaping into morphineville, I took her hand and watched the city's nightmare progress from absurdity to brutality on the little screen. I was too much "there" to be conscious of being content. But that's what I was. Content. No torment. No ecstasy or thrill. Just a calm, rippling peace. Like the wind-kissed lake in the Presidio.

Good Nightmare:

I'm in purgatory, sitting on a plush, fire-engine-red sofa in a sparsely furnished loft. The walls are concrete. I'm comfortable, but uneasy. I look around and notice a sign on the wall above a wooden rocking chair, its dark oak headrest carved into a bearded demon's head:

NOTICE:
TO EXPEDITE YOUR INTERVIEW WITH THE PRINCE OF DARKNESS. PLEASE REMAIN SITTING PATIENTLY. THE ANGEL OF DEATH WILL BE WITH YOU SHORTLY.

I understand. I'm dead and awaiting an interview with Satan to see if I'm worthy of spending eternity in damnation.

But I don't want to go to Hell. What kind of trick is this? How should I act? What can I do to outsmart Mephistopheles? I'm sure he's heard it all. Maybe if I just come clean and tell him I don't want to go to Hell, he'll realize that I'm too honest to be sent down. But maybe that's what he's expecting, and being stupid would be just the push to put me over the edge. I was stressed out. In my mind I kept attempting to develop elaborate ways that I could outsmart the Evil One. But it was no use. He was the master out-smarter. I began pacing the floor. I looked up and noticed various works of art depicting hellfire and the Devil himself. The waiting, along with an occasional glance at the paintings, tugged on me like unpaid parking tickets.

I glanced toward the opposite end of the loft and noticed a beautiful black girl. She looked about nineteen. Then it occurred to me. She was a nymph. Sort of a Devil's assistant to keep the customer's nerves intact. She was on her knees in just a thin cotton sundress. Her long, curly, mane flowed like water to the floor.

She had soft features with one thin eyebrow over both her black eyes. My stress dissolved into a molten desire. My mind went blank except for one thought: *I have to have her.* I walked over and stood next to her. She looked up and with a seductively lewd grin said in a gravelly drawl, "Hello, bad boy."

"I've got some time to kill," I said.

She remained on her knees, spread her legs, turned her head, and motioned with her hand toward her ass. I lifted her dress up over her shoulders, noticing the black hair under her arms and between her legs. I reached down and began rubbing her sex with my upturned fingers, the bottom, thick part of my palm pressing up against the fleshy opening of her rear. She swayed on all fours while her coal black ringlets fanned her arched back. She became wet. I undressed, crouched behind her, then entered her. She was tight and it took some effort. After just a few slow strokes, I turned her around, put myself back inside her and clasped her hands in mine.

As I lowered down to kiss her, I noticed that her front was a shade lighter than her back, like the hands of a black man. I was fucking a creature more beautiful than any human. I closed my eyes, curled my back, pushed deep inside her, and came. A sense of well-being, safety, and ultimate satisfaction warmed me.

But when I opened my eyes, my beautiful black nymph had transformed into a sleek sinewy panther. I froze, knowing that if I moved I would be ripped apart. But my fear quickly evaporated and I suddenly got the urge to strike the magnificent cat. I balled my hand into a fist and pounded the panther with all my strength on its powerful jaw. As it attacked, tearing at my flesh, I awoke.

I wondered if my mother had such dreams. In her morphine induced state, with the "infinite" number of cancer cells swimming in her brain, did she dream of sex and death? Did she even *think* of sex? Being so close to death did she in some frantic way reach back to memories of her past sexual life?

When I get sick from some mundane illness, the last thing on my mind is fucking. But now, so close to death, albeit indirectly through my mother, I couldn't get enough. I'd once heard one of my mother's lovers, a tall, good-looking Mexican harp player, refer to sex as "el pequeno muerte." The little death. The connection between death and sex is profound, but slippery. Are they siblings? Or are they closer, perhaps more of a child-parent relationship? Maybe master and slave?

Did this woman, who was desired by most men in earlier years, and who during the free love days of the 60s and early 70s slept with practically every man who crossed her path, have any sexual desire left? Laying in the spare bed in my mother's condo, a parade of her lovers began dancing in my memory: There was Louis Valentine, the black, eighteen-year-old quarterback for the local high school team. There was David Stockton, one of her college professors, a quiet, small man. She had confided in me about that one. "He couldn't get it up. He said there must be something wrong with me. I reached down and said, 'I'm wet—there's nothing wrong with *me*.'"

There was the surfing Mexican, Jorge Ramirez. Jorge was one of my mother's classmates. He was twenty-two, a little goofy, but built like *David*. He took me surfing a few times. There was the wholesale businessman Larry Capp, Bill the Malibu lifeguard, and Curt (I can't remember his last name), the Jewish stockbroker's son who lived with his mother in Brentwood. I liked Curt. He gave me home-grown pot that I smoked with my friends. One of my favorites was Tom Hostetler, a body-building actor. He rode a motorcycle, smoked a pipe, and wore thick glasses. My mother thought he was a chauvinist pig, but she adored him. He had a childlike enthusiasm for life within his macho veneer. In the 70s, he played the heavy in such classics as *Gone in 60 Seconds* and *Eat My Dust: Part Two.* He also appeared in *Playgirl* as "Mr. June." I once went to a play he was in: Treasure Island. He played a sinister but lovable Captain Hook. Last we heard, Tom married a woman he had gotten pregnant. He was the quintessential 70s player, but he had his code.

As Mom became more involved in her career, the men began to disappear.

She fell in love when she was in her forties with an activist attorney from Montana. Jerry Yellowbear was with the Oneida Nation and moved to California to practice constitutional law. He eventually ended up working for the Bureau of Indian Affairs. I never liked the guy. He took no interest in me or my sister and treated my mother like shit. He broke her heart when he called off the engagement and moved back to Montana. After that she wrote off men for the next seven or eight years and was just again beginning to open up to the possibility of romance when she became ill. She hadn't had sex for at least five years.

I lay in bed and thought of her. Thought how beautiful she was, and how I used to tell her I was going to marry a woman just like her. Of course I could never find one just like her. And now she was dying.

I couldn't fall back asleep. I needed to hear a friendly voice. One that wasn't connected to the situation. One that wasn't intimate with the details of chemotherapy or sluggish stools.

I phoned Sharon in San Francisco, hoping her husband or kids wouldn't answer.

"Hi, Sharon, it's Martin."

"Marty. How are you? How's your mom?"

"Not so good. She's fading fast. The doctor isn't giving her much time and her spirits are low."

"I'm sorry. Is there anything I can do?"

"You're doing it. I won't keep you, Sharon. I know it's late. I just wanted to call and thank you again for giving me this time off."

"There are more important things than work, Marty. Call me anytime if you need to, or want to, talk."

"Thanks, boss."

CHAPTER 18

Dr. Allen said he thought it best that she stay in the hospital for a time, which I took to mean until she died. I put up a front of an argument, but the truth was, emotionally and physically, I was drained. Months of attending to her every need had taken its toll. There were nights when I hardly slept. The coughing fits kept us both up. Sometimes in the middle of the night she would scream out as if in the midst of a bad dream. She was actually having momentary fits of consciousness. She would cry out in pain and terror when for a moment she'd feel her air supply cut off, or when she'd realize her predicament. In some respects she had accepted her fate. We talked about funeral arrangements, and we discussed her financial matters. But the intrepid brawler that occupied a portion of her psyche refused to accept anything less than domination. It had come out sporadically during her life, particularly in her childhood, after her father had died and all her family's anger was directed toward her.

Over time she had forgiven her mother for the beatings and the mental abuse, but she could never forgive her older brother.

He would punch her in the stomach, as not to leave marks. He would tie her up and take out his knife and threaten to cut her. The young Pablito had become a "vato." He ran with a group that called itself the East Side Boys. Once, he urinated in a Mason jar and poured its contents onto Laurita's bed when she was asleep. In the morning she woke up and thought she had wet the bed. She quietly began to clean up when her mother, tipped of a bedwetting incident by Pablito, entered the room and asked what she was doing. That beating took on added significance because her mother used her dead father's belt strap. The next day Laura jumped her brother, who pummeled her.

She had displayed that fighting, scrapping strength when her "tio," Manny, raped her in the back seat of his Ford sedan when she was fourteen. Running away to L.A. as a teenager, raising her kids alone, going to college and graduating with honors, these were all periods in which the dual-natured combatant had made its presence known.

A few months after she had been diagnosed and was camped out on a sofa after a debilitating chemo treatment, my father went to visit her. He offered her a joint and told her, "Remember how everyone thought you were nuts when you went back to school? Well, you did it and I knew then you could do it. You can do it again. You can beat it." But this time she was outmatched.

The day the doctor told me that my mother would be spending "time" in the hospital, my grandmother called and asked, "Should I come out now, Marty?"

I gave the usual, "No, not yet, grandma."

I don't know if she sensed it in my voice, or if she felt

death's breath, or if she just knew. But she refused to be put off. "I'm coming down, Martin." And so she stayed with me in my mother's condo until her daughter died.

For the first week, we'd get up, she'd make me breakfast, usually huevos and beans, along with cafe-con-leche, just like when I was little. Then we'd proceed glumly to the hospital. The old woman's stamina was Herculean. I had to drag her out of my mother's room nearly every night when visiting hours were over. Two nights during that first week she made me talk the nurse into letting us stay the night.

It was after that first week that the old familiar frantic feeling sneaked up on me. I had to get away. So I arranged a trip to San Francisco. One of my mother's friends agreed to take my grandmother to the hospital. She'd drop her off on the way to work and pick her up when she came home. I'd be gone just three days. I was sure my mother would hang on that long. After all these months it seemed a strange time to get away. No one questioned my decision, but I sensed a collective perplexity. Her friends, family, the doctors, they all knew that I wanted to be there when she died. Why take a chance now?

I told the friend staying at my apartment that I was coming home for the weekend. It just so happened he was taking a week-long trip to Seattle. Good.

I drove down on a Friday afternoon. I took Highway 5 until I reached the Central Valley, where I connected to 580. Then I took Interstate 80 to the Bay Bridge. It was overcast, but the drive on the upper deck heading into The City lifted my spirits. As the ferry tower and the waterfront came into view, as the downtown skyscrapers gathered depth, as the Golden Gate Bridge, Angel Island, and Alcatraz made their way into my sights, I forgot what I was driving away from. I felt embraced and welcomed home.

When I got to my apartment I sat on the chair near one

of the bay windows. I watched the turbulent, green water for what must have been an hour. I saw a ferry keeping time with the city's pulse lugging toward Sausalito. Sailboats and cruisers and barges came into and out of my view. Occasionally the cloud cover would open up teasing with a wisp of blue.

I had planned to spend the entire weekend alone, clearing out the incendiary devices that had ignited thoughts of death in my brain.

I laid down on the living room rug and listened to Elmore James' bottleneck guitar cry out my speakers: *You said you were hurtin', you almost lost your mind. Now the man you love, he hurt you all the time. But when things go wrong. . . wrong with you. . . it hurts me too. . .*

After a few hours I thought I'd check to see if there were any messages on the service. I'd called about a week ago, from the hospital. There was a message from Sarah, whom I hadn't spoken with since I learned my mother was sick. "Martin. Sarah. We haven't talked in a while. Call me."

That night we had coffee at the North Beach Cafe. I told her about my mother. "Death happens," she said with a mixture of empathy and bitterness. We lingered comfortably for about fifteen minutes before I got up the courage to ask about her father. "How long did it take your father to die?"

"He was diagnosed in June and he died the following February. He withered away to nothing after he was so sure that he was going to beat it. 'This is nothing compared to the death camp,' he joked. He was much stronger than I was. I cried myself to sleep every night for about a year."

I couldn't believe she was talking about it so calmly so I pressed on. "Did he suffer much?"

"Enough. I couldn't bring myself to go visit him the last

few weeks. I finally went to see him in the hospital the day he died. I leaned at his bedside and cried like a baby. I felt his hand on my head stroking my hair and when I looked up he was smiling at me. For that moment I felt okay. Later that hour he died in his sleep."

"Was your mother there?"

"That bitch? Thank God she didn't have the guts to show up. It would have been an insult."

"Oh?"

"She used to beat the shit out me, you know. But I could take that. It's the way she treated my father that turned me against her. And her broken promises."

We drank our coffee. I told her I was heading back in two days. As she stood to leave she grabbed my hand and squeezed with an intensity that communicated an inaccessible compassion. It also conveyed her attraction for me. She was still warm to my touch, though I had no inclination to pounce. Instead I sat and watched her walk away, letting her battered and thorny spirit fill me up.

Saturday morning.

Nothing like gambling to take your mind off things. They were running at Bay Meadows.

I drove down the peninsula on Highway 280, the Junipero Serra Freeway. I flashed my press pass and parked for free. It did the trick for admission as well.

With my Racing Form, program, Hav-a-Tampas, and pen, I found a box in the clubhouse and began studying.

The first race was an allowance for three-year-olds and older, non-winners of two races in the last year. It was six and a half furlongs on the dirt. I boxed three horses for a two dollar exacta: the two favorites and a gelding that went off at 8–1. The longshot had won a race a couple months back but hadn't done shit since finishing out of the money its last six races. The Form showed the horse had speed and its recent workouts were decent. I like to take chances with longshots, you make more money that way. It's more gratifying to pick a winner not too many people thought had a chance. If the horse broke well out of the gate it might hang on for first or second. It cost me twelve dollars to play all three horses to come in any combination for first and second. The two favorites came in. The long shot broke bad and finished out of the money. The exacta paid $13.20. So I was up a buck twenty after one race.

If the long shot had won with either of the favorites coming in second, I would have won about sixty dollars.

That's pretty much the way it went all day. I'd win a race, then lose three. The fourth race I hit for eighty dollars, but by the tenth and last race I was up only about three dollars.

I had a good feeling about the last race. It was a maiden, claiming race. None of the horses had won, or "broken their maiden." Anything can happen in a maiden race. Your best chance to hit a long shot is usually in a maiden race. I liked a horse named Lucky Daze, I just wasn't sure who to play him with. He was 4–1 on the morning line. He'd finished second in his two previous races. His workouts were good and the jockey had already won two races that day. I always bet a jock to win a third race. If he'd won two he'd usually put some extra effort into getting the hat trick. Handicappers at the track had seen this in the Form and were betting him down. He went off at 7–2. I still liked him despite the low odds.

I boxed him with two long shots: Diggers Delight and Laura's Lover.

Diggers Delight had never raced before. He was 10–1. He showed good work-outs, but his breeding was iffy and his stable had a low win percentage, thus the high odds. I played Laura's Lover on a hunch. If that horse came in and I hadn't bet him, I'd kick myself. If he didn't come in, at least I had given myself a chance to make some good money. He went off at 40–1. Lucky Daze was the three horse. Diggers Delight was the five, and Laura's Lover was the seven.

All three horses got off to a good start. I was encouraged. But it was a long race, a mile and a 16th on the turf. At the quarter pole, Diggers Delight led but the field was bunched up. The favorite, Lucky Daze was third, only a horse length back, and Laura's Lover was in the middle of the pack about five lengths off the pace. Half way around, Lucky Daze began to make his move, sprinting wide, gaining on the front runner with each stride. Diggers Delight had fallen back out of contention and Laura's Lover was on the rail in fifth, four lengths back.

At that point I didn't have much faith since Laura's Lover had never shown that he was a closer. As the horses approached the stretch it looked like Lucky Daze was going to pull away and win for fun, but then I heard the track announcer call the seven horse. . . "And from the middle of the pack. . . HEERE COMES LAURA'S LOVER LOOKING TO PULL OFF THE UPSET!!" Halfway down the stretch it was a two horse race with both jockeys whipping furiously. Lucky Daze was two lengths ahead but Laura's Lover was moving up fast. With about two hundred yards to go, they were neck and neck. I started screaming as I watched through my binoculars. "GET 'EM SEVEN. . . GET 'EM SEVEN. . . COME ON, PICK IT UP. GET 'EM SEVEN!" The track announcer was in a frenzy. "IT'S LUCKY DAZE AND LAURA'S LOVER DOWN TO THE WIRE LUCKY DAZE. . . LAURA'S LOVER. . . LUCKY DAZE. . . LAURA'S LOVER. . . AND AT THE WIRE." He paused before going out on a limb "IT APPEARS LAURA'S LOVER HAS PULLED OFF THE UPSET VICTORY BY A NOSE!"

It was a photo finish, but unless my eyesight was playing tricks and the track announcer had blown the call, Laura's Lover had head-bobbed a win. We were told to hold all tickets until the results were official. I had won regardless but if the longshot had pulled it off, the difference would be the difference between an okay day and a great day. It seemed forever until the results hit the tote board. There was a collective moan from the crowd with a smattering of cheers when the results were announced. Sure enough, Laura's Lover had won. The exacta paid $440.20.

It was only fitting. I'd picked up gambling from my father, who was still a hundred times the handicapper I was. He had taken my mother to Santa Anita for their honeymoon. She was young and happy just being with him. She would come to despise the track though, blaming gambling in part for their breakup. Both parents came through for me in that tenth race. It seemed strange that anything connected with my mother would help me to win a horse race, but one never questions the race gods, just thanks them.

I cashed in my ticket and went home.

CHAPTER 19

Upon my return to L.A., Dr. Allen informed me that my mother could die "any day now." He had transferred her to Holy Cross Villa, essentially a hospice unit in the hills above the valley.

Three days later she died. According to the death certificate she took her last breath at ten minutes past three in the morning. I was asleep in her condo. My grandmother had stayed in her hospital room. She called me immediately. "Momma's gone, Marty."

I called my sister then went to the hospital.

When we walked into the room, my grandmother was sitting next to my mother's bed, rubbing her lifeless, yellow face. I walked over to my grandmother and took her small, wrinkled hand and held it tight. She stood up, embraced me around my chest and began sobbing. "Don't burn her, Marty! Please Marty, don't burn her!"

I stroked her forehead and her gray, braids and comforted her the best I could.

My mother was wearing her paisley scarf and a half smile. Her eyes were closed. I wondered if she had died that peacefully or if the nurses had shut her eyes. My grandmother said that she "passed" while sleeping soundly.

We left my sister alone with my mother for a few minutes then my grandmother and I went back into the room. I stood next to the bed and touched my mother's forehead. It was cold. I looked at her face and tried to convince myself that she was better off. But something about her expression left me wondering. I wanted my goodbye to be something profound or poetic but as I opened my mouth to speak all that came out was, "I'll see you soon."

When the man from the mortuary came to pick up her body, my grandmother broke down. She kept repeating, "No, no, no! Laurita! No, no."

I had to forcefully walk her out of the room while the corpse was put in the black, plastic zip-up bag.

I drove home with my grandmother back to my mother's condo. After I helped her to bed, I sat on the couch, the same piece of furniture that my mother had spent her last months on, and watched the sunrise. I studied the different colors: first the black of a cloudless night, then the dim white of the distant sun which had yet to float up over the horizon, and finally the full explosion of the blinding orange, greeting all, the living and the dead, and everyone else. In a matter of minutes, the sun's rays burst through the smog and it was hot again. I picked up the phone and dialed Sarah's number.

Her scratchy, sleepy voice answered, "Hello?"

"Hi."

"Martin?"

"Yes, it's Martin."

"Is she dead?"

"She died about three hours ago."

"And you need me."

"Like the sun."

"Are you having a funeral?"

"It's all arranged. A memorial service Monday and the cremation on Wednesday."

"I'll be there tomorrow."

CHAPTER 20

To be loved means to be consumed in flames,
to love is to give light with inexhaustible oil.
To be loved is to pass away; to love is to endure.

Rainer Maria Rilke

The graveyard was well groomed; old fashioned with hundreds of headstones scattered on the receding hillside under the dangling cypress twigs. Sparse patches of grass crept up from between the trees and graves, each leaf posturing for its own minuscule bit of dirt. It was healthy, fragrant grass, but over the last months had been bleached a wheatlike pale green by the scorching summer sun. There was no smog and the sky above the hills of the cemetery was a vivid blue. The temperature had cooled with a slight breeze from the north, making it seem more like spring than summer. I wore a light green windbreaker over a black T-shirt. Plenty of people had attended the memorial service, maybe two hundred, but on this day it was just Sarah and me.

The family-owned-and-operated cemetery was one of only four in all of Los Angeles that did cremations. The funeral director at our mortuary said that most people don't attend the cremation, implying to me that they were done assembly-line style. Like a bread factory, once an oven is empty, throw in another loaf.

It didn't smell like death on the cemetery grounds. The fresh grass, the dirt, the dull, woody aroma of the oak brought back memories of baseball. I'd always loved the smell of the diamond, whether playing or watching. As a boy, Dodger Stadium was my shrine, but any back lot field did the trick.

A thin, pleasant-looking woman greeted us at the cemetery entrance. She was wearing black jeans, simple black cowboy boots, and a silk, flower-patterned red blouse. Deep lines in her face betrayed her years, and her long, curly hair was light brown. She smiled and escorted us to the front office. We sat down at her desk and she began explaining the procedure. We would be taken to the crematorium where I would be allowed to ID my mother.

The body would then be placed in the oven. It would take about ten minutes before they turned off the furnace and let the ashes cool. Afterward they would grind any bone fragments, and along with the ashes, put them in the urn of my choice. She displayed a variety of containers. I chose the cheapest because my sister and I planned to scatter her ashes over a mountaintop near San Francisco.

The one time my mother had visited me up north, we hiked that mountain. She was taken by its majestic view and expansive grass and poppy-blanketed hilltop. It would be a good spot for her, the mountain named *Tamal-Pais* or Ocean View by the Miwoks.

I listened closely as the cemetery woman continued her

explanation. Halfway through she glanced at Sarah then, asked me if I was holding up all right. "I'm okay," I answered.

The woman and a burly, mustached cemetery worker, whom she introduced as her brother Rick, led us to the crematorium.

Inside on a cast-iron table my mother's body lay. She was in a cardboard casket. The woman studied my reaction as we entered the cement structure. She looked into my eyes as if questioning, *Can you handle this?* Then she asked if I wanted to identify the body. I nodded and Sarah put her arm around me.

My mother looked as she did the day she died. Her eyes were closed and on her bald head was that paisley scarf. The half smile remained frozen on her face. The woman's brother put the lid back on the box and wheeled the iron table to an adjacent room. Inside were three brick ovens, all joined by thick iron frames. Each oven had metal semi circle doors with small brass handles. The doors were slightly open revealing pilot flames flickering deep inside. Sarah and I stood arm in arm on the cool, clay ground not ten feet from the furnaces. My mother's body, still on the iron gurney, was brought over and lined up headfirst with the middle oven.

The woman's brother opened the doors and slid the cardboard box into its cavernous opening. He shut the doors and turned the furnace up to its highest setting. The round plastic temperature control knob was much like the one on my grandmother's old gas oven.

The heat quickly warmed the room as the stifled roars of the flames, like those first few moments of an earthquake, began to unsettle the nerves of all present. I stood my ground initially, not allowing myself to feel anything. Something inside me was attempting to turn on the objective reporter switch, but that light didn't come on. Instead, as the flames began to reach my mother's flesh I suddenly lost all my strength. My body was becoming limp. The numbness made its way down my head, then my neck and shoulders, then my arms. As my head slumped, my legs went weak. Sarah, feeling my collapse, held tight and propped me up. The mortician noticed and motioned toward her brother. They looked at each other and the woman said I should leave. *I've come this far*, I thought, *I'll see it through.*

I mustered the strength to stand erect and say firmly, "I'm fine." But within thirty seconds I collapsed again. I remained conscious however, aware in an odd, detached way. Movement and speech seemed unnecessary and stupid. I was vaguely aware of what was happening outside of me, but it was distant and of no concern. The lady mortician insisted that I be removed from the crematorium. Sarah demanded that I stay and told the brother to bring me something to sit on. He wheeled over the ash ridden gurney from near the oven.

Then I was inside the middle furnace with my dead mother. At first I felt panic and fear. I heard a high-pitched howl echoing around me. It was my howling! I felt the flames begin to engulf me, the burning heat lapping around and through me. And then I was my mother. We had merged. Consciousness was consciousness but within the merger was a separation, like when you slice soft butter. I felt a resistance. My mother was refusing to leave.

She was dead and her body had been destroyed but she was clinging to life with an excruciating tenacity, groping desperately to *my* life force. I could hear my screams, muted, but binding me to the world of the living. In between wails I heard my voice comforting my mother. Quickly but softly I was saying, "It's okay. It's okay. It's okay. It's okay."

Then a brilliant image enveloped my consciousness: a copper-skinned Indian, clothed only in moccasins and breechcloth below an elevated funeral bed. He had a white lightning bolt painted on his face from his forehead to his chin and one eagle feather strung off his tied-back black hair. He was chanting and howling a deep wolf's cry as he danced around the flaming heap which was spewing black smoke into a white desert sky.

Then blackness. No flames. No howling. I was aware of nothing. I saw nothing. I heard nothing. As nothingness faded I saw a sphere of light on my mind's black horizon. At first I felt a calm warmth which quickly transformed into a comfortable ecstasy, then finally into something I had been on the edge of many times, but never fully experienced: pure joy.

I'd caught glimpses of it. That morning with Sarah, winning big at the track, or waking to a sunrise in the Sierra. But always it was tainted with the knowledge that it was temporary. In that moment, sitting on that iron gurney far away, I had no such knowledge, no such burden. Time was immaterial, unknown, and unimaginable. Oh, the pure joy of perpetual ecstasy!

Then I questioned it. *What was this? How could I maintain it? How do I possess this? It's her! She knows! I'll find her and stay with her! She'll lead me there!*

And awareness became contaminated by pursuit.

As quickly as my mother had vanished, she was back, but now serene and imageless. With the essence of a content smile she conveyed her peace and gave me back my breath. *Not now, Marty. It's not time.* I felt her say, *listen.* And in the distance I heard a faint echo. "Marty. Marty?"

****

I felt a warmth on my neck and opened my eyes. Sarah was leaning down, holding my head in her arms. "You're back. Thank God, you're back."

As my earthly surroundings came into focus it was as if my powers of awareness were for the first time fully alive. My sense of smell was layered. Foremost was Sarah. I could smell the mixture of her natural, sweet must, combined with the lavender soap she always bought in Chinatown. Beyond that was the dusty, burnt smell of the ash and bone. Floating around that was the smell of damp grass from the graveyard, distant and alive. I breathed it all in with a new-found amazement. As I looked up at Sarah, with her hair gently falling over her shoulders and her eyes filled with compassion and concern, her beauty overwhelmed me.

As I stood up, I felt strong and alert. The mortician and her brother observed me with trepidation. "Are you all right?" asked the woman.

"I feel great. Thanks for asking," and I chuckled.

But Sarah knew. She showed no apprehension. She was swept in. She took my hand and suggested that we walk while we waited for the ashes to cool. As I left the crematorium, the colors and depth of the graveyard appeared more vivid than before. Sarah walked me over to a bench. We sat in silence for many minutes as I let my senses drink in everything. I picked up an oak leaf and studied its translucent veins. It intrigued and fascinated me. I noticed the olive-colored stem and deep green of its thin flesh and felt compelled to eat it. I chewed then swallowed. Sarah looked at me with baffled amusement.

Then a bird began singing. "Do you hear that?" I asked.

"What?"

"It's a finch and its singing for us. I think it's Patsy Cline."

"You're nuts."

"No, really. It's a little sing songy, but if you listen closely you can pick up the melody. . . *I fall to pieces each time I see you again. I fall to pieces how can I be just your friend. You want me to act like we've never kissed, you want me to forget, pretend we never met. And I cried and I cried, but I haven't yet. You walk by and I fall to pieces.* Do you hear it?"

"Yeah, I do." And she laughed. "Patsy Cline, huh?"

"I have to make love to you right now."

"I know just the place." She walked me over to the wooden building that housed the office. In the back, around from the entrance of the cemetery, was a door. She opened it and took me inside. It was a bathroom, unlike one would expect to find at such a place. It had a large, old-fashioned bathtub. The tile floor was spotless and shiny. To the right of the oak-seated toilet was a porcelain sink. Carved into the clover shaped faucet handles were a calligraphic C and H. Sarah shut the door then took my face in her hands. She kissed me and ran her fingers up into my hair.

I lifted her up on to the sink and slid my right arm up her dress, the same earthy sundress she had worn in Sonoma. I felt the roundness of her small belly, then moved up to the place between her breasts. She was smooth and delicate and just a bit damp from perspiration. Then I gripped her breasts hard and fast while I leaned up and sucked her neck.

I moved my mouth down, nuzzling and kissing her flesh through her dress. When I got to her knees, I slowly licked the inside of her leg and made small circles with my tongue on her stubbly skin as I continued down to her sandals. Then in one long motion, I went up her calf, inched up her thigh and beyond. She breathed in deeply. With the tip of my tongue inside her, I moved my head so that the back of my tongue rubbed strategically. Her ass began bouncing on the porcelain and she came while her hands massaged my head. I looked up and her eyes twitched with desire. I stood up, kicked off my boots, and pulled down my jeans.

She reached down and grabbed me with both hands as she wrapped her legs around my waist. I twisted her hair at the scalp in my palms and fingertips as her mouth pleaded for, then accepted, my tongue. Never in my life had I felt more aware. More at peace. More alive. As we transfixed a rapturous gaze on each other's eyes only our breathing was necessary. The past and the future were nowhere to be found.

Afterward I picked up Sarah's panties, squeezing the soft silk up to my face before slipping them in my back pocket. As we walked hand in hand to the front office to gather my mother's remains, Sarah leaned over and whispered in my ear, "Te quiero, mijo. Te quiero."

SCOTT LETTIERI has had numerous short stories and poems published in such publications as *The Poetry Review* and *Santa Barbara Literary Journal*. He's written a book of short stories entitled *Waking Hours*. He has a BA degree in journalism and currently is a news reporter at CNET Radio in San Francisco. *Sinner's Paradise* is his first novel.